Maddie pivoted to face him.

"You need a place to live that allows dogs. I need a maintenance person. I can't afford to pay much, but I can offer you the barn loft and three meals a day."

Witt's jaw dropped. "Are you sure about this? Because you barely know a thing about me, and—"

"I know you love dogs, and I saw yesterday how hard you'll work to finish a job." She hesitated, the tiniest flicker of doubt making her glance away briefly. Then she hiked her chin. "Please. Say yes before I realize what an absurd idea this is and change my mind."

Kneeling, he called his dog over and pressed Ranger's face between his hands. "What do you think, boy? Should we accept this lady's kind offer before she comes to her senses?"

Ranger yipped and licked Witt's nose.

"I'll take that as a yes." He stood and extended his right hand to Maddie. "You're an answer to my prayers, Ms. McNeill. In more ways than you can possibly imagine."

Award-winning author **Myra Johnson** writes emotionally gripping stories about love, life and faith. She is a two-time finalist for the ACFW Carol Award and winner of the 2005 RWA Golden Heart® Award. Married since 1972, Myra and her husband have two married daughters and seven grandchildren. She and her husband reside in Texas, sharing their home with two pampered rescue dogs.

Visit the Author Profile page at LoveInspired.com.

A Steadfast Companion

Myra Johnson

LOVE INSPIRED
INSPIRATIONAL ROMANCE

LOVE INSPIRED®
INSPIRATIONAL ROMANCE

Recycling programs
for this product may
not exist in your area.

ISBN-13: 978-1-335-58556-1

A Steadfast Companion

Copyright © 2023 by Myra Johnson

For questions and comments about the quality of this book, please contact us
at CustomerService@Harlequin.com.

Love Inspired
22 Adelaide St. West, 41st Floor
Toronto, Ontario M5H 4E3, Canada
www.LoveInspired.com

Printed in U.S.A.

Bless the Lord, O my soul,
And forget not all his benefits: Who redeemeth
thy life from destruction; who crowneth thee
with lovingkindness and tender mercies;
Who satisfieth thy mouth with good things;
so that thy youth is renewed like the eagle's.
—*Psalm* 103:2, 4–5

For dog lovers everywhere, especially those who offer loving sanctuary and a forever home to displaced or unadoptable senior canines. Also with gratitude to my Montana daughter, Johanna, for her insights and research assistance.

Chapter One

She couldn't put it off any longer.

Not with eight inches of snow predicted and the kennel roof damaged from a broken tree branch. Twenty-plus dogs were counting on her, most of them seniors, others with chronic ailments that had rendered them unadoptable.

"Hi, yes, it's Maddie McNeill. Thanks for returning my call." Cell phone pressed to her ear, Maddie gazed out the kitchen window of the old farmhouse as a pewter sky closed in. Those were definitely snow clouds. "Do you know Elk Valley?"

"Out Interstate 90 northwest of Missoula, right?" The kindly male voice belonged to a handyman named Witt. First name? Last name? Maddie wasn't sure. She'd found him on the hire-a-repairman website her veterinarian and closest friend, Julia Frasier, had recommended. He was the soonest available at the lowest rate.

And she needed both.

"Yes, pass Frenchtown, then take the Elk Valley Road exit. Go about six miles north, then take a right at the Elk Valley mini-mall." She gave him a couple more turn directions, then told him to watch for Eventide Dog Sanctuary. "The sign's not very big, and we're off the road about a quarter mile. Follow the lane to the kennels. I'll be watching for you."

"Yes, ma'am, see you in…" He paused, probably checking his GPS. "About forty-eight minutes, give or take."

Disconnecting, Maddie breathed deeply in an attempt to settle her jittery stomach. She didn't like depending on other people, least of all strangers. But one thing she'd been forced to admit since inheriting the sanctuary from her late grandmother was that she couldn't do it all herself.

She twisted her long mop of strawberry-blond curls beneath a knit winter hat and donned her grandmother's faded denim barn coat. The plaid flannel lining still carried the scent of Nana's handmade lavender-and-lemon soap. Eyes closed, Maddie inhaled the calming fragrance and wished for one more day with the woman who'd raised her.

No use dwelling on the past when the very real present awaited, along with all its inherent problems. Not that she considered the dogs a *problem*, or Nana's two gentle horses either. The difficulty lay in how to manage everything. Food. Vet bills. Facility maintenance. Utilities. Insurance. One expense after another, and so little sanctuary support coming in, mainly from the grants and donors Nana already had in place. When those ran out, or if people stopped giving, then what? The animals deserved better. They deserved the same loving care Nana had given Maddie when her own mother couldn't be counted on.

She stepped out the back door into a biting north

wind. Not unusual for April in Montana, but Maddie was ready for spring. A real spring, with abundant sunshine and myriad flowers in bloom. Living in Southern California for fifteen years while teaching English at a small private university, she'd been spoiled by the milder climate. Here in the foothills of the Northern Rockies, springtime highs could fluctuate anywhere from the thirties to the eighties, and only the hardiest blossoms dared to show their pretty faces. Maddie's childhood favorites had always been the sunny yellow buttercups and the dazzling pink shooting stars.

In the kennel, the dogs greeted her with happy barks. While she waited for the handyman, she freshened water bowls and handed out homemade sweet-potato treats. After several belly rubs and ear scratches, she gave each dog an extra blanket. The underfloor heating system was usually sufficient on even the coldest nights, but the arthritic dogs especially welcomed a bit more warmth and comfort. On the other hand, if the handyman couldn't fix the roof in time, Maddie might end up taking all the dogs into the house with her tonight.

The rumble of an engine drew her outside, where a rusty off-white vehicle pulled up in front of the kennel. It was one of those mini-trucks some city folks chose just so they could claim to drive a pickup. This one looked—and sounded—like it had seen better days.

An average-looking, fiftyish guy in a baseball cap and tan corduroy coat emerged from the cab. He lifted a hand in greeting. "Ms. McNeill? I'm Witt, from Happy's Helpers. So you've got a roof problem?"

Nodding, she gestured toward the near left corner of the kennel roof. "It was damaged by a tree limb.

With the amount of snow they're predicting, I'm worried about my dogs."

"Absolutely. Let's go take a look." His genuine smile matched his voice on the phone earlier. "Do you have a ladder, or should I bring mine from the truck?"

She glanced at the shiny aluminum ladder peeking over the tailgate. It looked a lot sturdier than the rickety wooden contraption that was Nana's. "Better bring yours."

The man wanted to check the underside of the roof first, so Maddie showed him inside the kennel. He set up his ladder beneath the small, square attic door and hoisted himself through. Cautious footsteps overhead and the occasional sweep of a flashlight beam across the opening traced his path.

He returned to the opening and knelt to peer down at Maddie. "Besides the tree limb damage, it looks like you've had some roof leaks. A couple of these rafters show evidence of wood rot and should be replaced. Some of the insulation, too."

This was turning into a much bigger—and more expensive—job than she'd hoped. "Can you maybe just patch it for now, enough to get me through till summer?"

Heaving a sigh, Witt lowered himself through the opening and descended the ladder. "Ma'am, that wouldn't be wise or safe."

"I know. It's just…" Arms folded, she worried her lower lip.

He nodded thoughtfully, then knelt and reached through the wire mesh kennel gate to scratch Joey's chin. The scruffy white German shepherd mix slitted his eyes and groaned with pleasure. "Aren't you a handsome boy?"

"Well, now you've made a friend for life."

Witt gave a soft, sad chuckle. "They don't call 'em man's best friend for nothing."

He straightened, and for the first time since his arrival, she looked directly at him. His dusky brown eyes held a story, one she guessed would take a long, long time to tell, and much of it, not unlike those of some of the dogs in her care, would probably be hard to hear.

Abruptly, she tore her gaze away. "How much can you do before this weather front blows in? Because if the kennel isn't safe, I'll have to figure out something else for my dogs, and—"

"I'll get you through tonight's snowstorm, at the very least." Jaw firm, he scanned the water-spotted ceiling. "I'll need to run to the builders' supply for a few things. Unless you have any scrap wood you can spare. I'll likely need to replace some shingles up top, too."

"There's wood and leftover shingles in the barn, I think." She motioned toward the door.

He maintained a polite distance as he followed her across the driveway to the big white barn. Inside, Sunny and Sage nickered from their stalls. After pointing Witt to the storeroom where odds and ends got stashed, Maddie found a couple of Starlight mints in her pocket and gave one to each of the horses.

Shortly, Witt emerged from the storeroom with a stack of shingles and an armload of graying two-by-fours in various lengths. "These'll do fine. I'll get started, if that's all right with you."

"Yes, please." Anxious to get the repairs underway, Maddie held open the barn door for him. The shingles were from when Nana'd had the barn reroofed a few years ago, so it was in good shape. The house roof, too, or so Maddie hoped. She couldn't afford more repair bills.

Outside, the wind gusted, and the sky had darkened even more. She shivered and tugged her collar close around her neck. Tiny white flakes were already speckling her coat sleeves. She hoped Witt could finish before the snow began in earnest.

He sidled through the kennel entrance and laid the supplies in the aisle. "I'll be working directly over the two dog runs on this end. You should move those fellas till I'm done."

"There aren't any empty runs. I can put them in the kitchen." She nodded toward the small adjoining room where she prepared the dogs' meals.

Witt searched for something in his toolbox. "So your sanctuary's full up?"

"It pretty much stays that way. Dogs come here without much hope, so I do my best to give them a happy and comfortable forever home. Usually the only time there's a vacancy is when…" She finished with a shrug.

He gave an understanding nod, then cleared his throat roughly. "Well, it's a fine and decent thing you're doing here."

"I'd expand if I had the wherewithal. But as it is, I can barely afford to stay open for these guys." An aching lump formed in Maddie's throat as she glimpsed the curious furry faces peeking through the gates on either side of the aisle. "And I can't—I *won't*—give up on them."

Witt felt bad he couldn't promise more than a patch job before the snow arrived. But one look at the sky as they'd crossed from the barn to the kennel and he could tell they were on borrowed time. The woman's dedication to the dogs touched something deep inside him, and he'd do as much as he could to help her protect them. If only he could believe his longtime pal Ranger had ended up with someone as caring as Maddie McNeill.

Last time he'd seen the sweet old mutt was more than two years ago. Delirious with fever from a near-fatal bout of pneumonia, he'd watched helplessly from the back of an ambulance while an animal control officer wrestled the whining, anxious dog into a crate. Once Witt was out of the hospital, then completed a stint in rehab, enough time had passed that if Ranger hadn't been adopted by someone else, he'd probably been put down. As it turned out, the men's transitional home where Witt had been accepted didn't allow pets anyway.

While he measured and cut boards to shore up the damaged section of roof, his gaze continually drifted to Maddie. Wisps of pale copper curls had escaped her nubby knit hat. She had a fair complexion, lightly freckled across the bridge of her prettily turned-up nose. When the light caught her eyes just right, they shimmered like an azure summer sky.

He wasn't a good judge of a woman's age, but the crinkles around her eyes made him think fortysomething, possibly only a little younger than his fifty-one years. Her concern for the dogs was enough to make him like her, even if she did seem kind of skittish. If she lived alone this far from town—and he hadn't seen signs of anyone else around—he could understand her unease about having a strange man on the premises. Which was why he'd done his best to appear friendly and nonthreatening.

She'd gone to the house for a few minutes and returned with a thermos and a chipped mug. She filled the mug with a dark and aromatic brew, then offered it to Witt as he measured a board. "Thought you could use something hot to drink."

"Thanks. I never turn down coffee." Taking a careful sip, he eyed the dusting of snow on her cap and shoulders. "How's it looking out there?"

"Not good. How much longer till you're done?"

He wished he could say soon, but the roof was in worse shape than he'd first thought. He replied with a grimace and a shrug.

Obviously not the answer she was hoping for. Mouth tight, she closed her eyes briefly. "I can't ask you to keep working. The roads will be getting worse by the minute, so you should head home while you can."

"But the dogs—"

"I'll take them to the house."

Witt had counted twenty-four runs. Which meant twenty-four dogs in various stages of declining health and ability. He cast her a doubtful frown. "All of them?"

"I'll manage. It won't be the first time."

He gulped the rest of his coffee, then set down the empty mug and reached for his hammer and another piece of wood. "If it's all the same to you, I'd rather keep at it. If it doesn't look like I can finish in the next couple of hours, I'll help you get the dogs to the house before I leave."

"I can't ask you to do that. You really should—"

"Ma'am," he said as pleasantly as possible, "it's not up for debate. I'm not deserting you or these dogs, and that's final."

He couldn't fix what he'd done wrong in the past, but he'd made a promise to God and himself that he'd never let anyone down again. Least of all a pretty, red-haired woman with a heart for the forgotten and undervalued creatures of this world. He'd been there himself not so long ago. If someone hadn't had compassion for him, if they hadn't looked beyond the brokenness of a derelict living under a bridge and seen something in him worth saving, he might not be around today to mend this roof. And who knew if Ms. Maddie McNeill would have found anyone else willing to make a forty-mile trip to practically the middle of nowhere with an April snowstorm threatening?

He'd done what he could in the attic. With the rafters and roof panels reinforced, now he had a bit more confidence climbing onto the roof to replace the damaged shingles—provided the moaning north wind cooperated. Teeth chattering, he dropped through the attic opening and climbed down the ladder into the much warmer kennel aisle.

Maddie turned from peering out the narrow window in the door. "You stayed too long. You'll never make it out to the road, much less all the way back to Missoula. I'm sorry, I shouldn't have let you—"

"It was my choice, one hundred percent." Fingerless gloves made gripping tools and nails easier but didn't protect icy fingertips. Witt refilled his mug from the coffee thermos and let the warmth seep into his hands. The ham-and-cheese sandwich he'd had for lunch was wearing off, but it might be all he got until he made it back to town. At the rate it was snowing out there, whether that would be tonight or tomorrow or two days from now was anyone's guess.

Yep, he'd made his choice, and now he was stuck with it. They both were.

After several swallows of coffee, he'd begun to thaw

out. Which made the idea of leaving this cozy kennel and venturing onto the roof extremely unpleasant. Just a few shingles replaced, though, and the dogs would be good for the night. That'd make it all worthwhile. Then maybe Ms. McNeill wouldn't mind him camping out in one of her barn stalls. Horses gave off quite a bit of body heat, after all.

Steeling himself, he stocked his tool belt with hammer and nails, then stowed the ladder under one arm. With the other, he hefted the stack of shingles and started for the door.

Maddie's jaw dropped. Hands raised, she blocked the way. "You can't go up there now. It's too dangerous."

"This'll be the easy part." He hoped. "Ten minutes and I'm done."

She still looked doubtful, but after a moment's consideration, she stepped aside and opened the door. He hadn't expected her to follow him out into this weather, but she did. When she steadied the ladder without his asking, he wouldn't deny his gratitude.

Using his coat sleeve to brush aside the snow, he quickly determined which shingles needed replacing. He snapped off what he could reach of the weaker branches from the offending tree, then made quick work of patching the roof.

Fingers growing numb again, he dropped to the ground. "There, almost as good as new. Once this weather clears, I can come back and make permanent repairs."

"I—I'll have to let you know." She looked away and whisked snowflakes off her eyelashes. "How much do I owe you for today?"

As he folded the ladder, he nodded toward the kennel door. "Mind if we talk about that where it's warmer?"

Back inside, he got his work order tablet from the toolbox. According to the Happy's Helpers associates app on his phone, he'd spent about four hours on the job, which included the drive out, and he could add on another forty-five minutes for the return trip. Based on the rate he'd quoted, the app calculated the amount due.

Witt eyed the figure, then glanced at Maddie. Shifting from foot to foot, she chewed her lower lip. She gripped a checkbook like she could choke it to death.

Remember, Witt, "The labourer is worthy of his reward." The line from First Timothy was a favorite of Carl Anderson's, his counselor at the transitional home. *If you don't acknowledge your God-given value, how can you expect others to respect you?*

Easier said than done, in Witt's case. Besides, it didn't take a mind reader to surmise the dog sanctuary was struggling, and it made his gnawingly empty stomach hurt even worse to ask Ms. McNeill to stretch her slim budget any further. Problem was, the handyman service would take their cut of the actual total no matter what. And Witt had less than two months to put aside enough money for a rental deposit on his own place before his time was up at the transitional home.

If he didn't succeed—

Dear God, I've come this far. Please don't let me end up on the streets again.

Maddie held her breath as she waited for Witt to give her the total. He frowned and scratched his head and squinted at his phone so long that she wondered if maybe he'd forgotten his reading glasses.

She ventured closer. "Is there a problem?"

"No, I'm…ah…just calculating your discount."

"My discount?" That was unexpected.

"Yeah, last job on a Friday always means ten percent off. So it comes to…" He tapped some buttons on his phone, then read her the amount. "Make it payable to Happy's Helpers, then put 'Witt' in the memo."

Since when did a repair business give discounts for the last job on a Friday? Usually they wanted extra if the work bled into their weekend, but she wasn't about to argue. She wrote the check, then tore it out and handed it to him. "I appreciate all you did, but now you'll never make it back to Missoula tonight. About all I can offer is a hot meal and a place to sleep. There's a room over the barn where a hired man used to stay. It hasn't been used in a while, but it has heat and plumbing."

Witt shot her a grateful smile. "That's more than I could have asked for or expected. Thank you."

"You should go on up and get the heater cranking. As soon as I settle the dogs for the night, I'll start supper and find some bedding and towels for you."

"I can help with the dogs." A wistful look filled those shadowed eyes. "In fact, I'd enjoy it."

She could hardly say no to a man who'd proven so kind and accommodating. With a shrug, she showed him into the kennel kitchen. A whiteboard over the counter listed each dog's diet, so it was easy enough to get him started filling kibble bowls while she returned the two displaced dogs to their runs, then meted out medications and supplements. With both of them working, they finished quickly.

After the dogs had eaten and taken care of business, Maddie instructed Witt on how she cleaned the runs and disposed of waste. That done, she gave the kennel one last check, then bade the dogs good-night and dimmed the overhead lights.

Bracing herself for the blowing snow, she zipped up her coat. Witt did the same. They tromped through foot-deep drifts to the barn, where Maddie fed the horses and refreshed the shavings in their stalls. Outside again, she pointed Witt to the wooden stairs next to the barn door. "The loft's unlocked. After you get the heater going, come on to the house while the room warms up."

His brows drew together. He gave his head a doubt-ful shake. "That's your home, ma'am. I can't impose."

"And I can't let you freeze to death. It's too cold out here to argue. I'll expect you at my kitchen door in ten minutes." Snow blurring her vision, she bustled across the yard.

After leaving her coat, cap and boots in the mudroom and shaking out her tangled hair, she padded in sock feet to the pantry in search of something she could serve a cold and hungry handyman. Canned chili and beans would do the trick. She found a box of corn muffin mix, too. By the time she had the chili on the stove and muf-fins in the oven, she glimpsed Witt slogging through the snow toward the back door. She tapped on the win-dow over the sink and signaled him to let himself in.

Shortly, he stepped in from the mudroom. He looked different without his jacket and baseball cap, and the sight of a man in her kitchen—a rather handsome, clean-shaven man, graying at the temples—made her heart stammer.

She roughly cleared her throat and turned to stir the chili. "Supper's cooking. Bathroom's down the hall if you'd like to wash up. I've got to run down to the basement and tend to a couple more dogs."

Witt gave a disbelieving laugh. "You have *more* dogs?"

"These have special needs, so I keep them close."

"If there's anything I can do—"

"Give the chili a stir, if you would. And make sure the corn muffins don't burn. I set a timer, but my oven gets a little flaky." At the basement door, she smiled over her shoulder. "Thanks. I shouldn't be long."

Maybe she should be more uncomfortable about allowing a strange man into her house, much less leaving him upstairs while she ventured alone to the basement. At least if he followed her down and wanted to try anything, the rear corner of the basement was on a downhill slope and she could escape into the fenced backyard.

"You're being paranoid," she muttered. If Witt had evil intentions toward her, he could just as easily have acted on them in the kennel or the barn.

A soft whimper came from the dog crate across from the steps. Poor little Phoebe, an eleven-year-old bichon frise mix, had come to the sanctuary with a case of ringworm, large bald patches marring her fluffy white coat. Meds and ointments had helped tremendously, and hopefully in another few days Maddie could start socializing Phoebe with other dogs her size.

Once she'd seen to the little dog's needs, she washed her hands at the basement sink, then prepared a bowl of food for her other problem dog. Every day for the past five months, she'd hoped in vain for a breakthrough with the reclusive creature who could rarely be coaxed from the farthest corner of his pen. He'd come to the sanctuary with no collar and no history, other than that he'd been found running loose in downtown Missoula about a year ago. When the no-kill shelter where he'd been taken had declared him unadoptable because of his chronic depression and withdrawal, her friend Julia, who volunteered veterinary services for the shelter, suggested they call Maddie.

Julia guessed the black-and-tan dog to be part German shepherd, possibly with some kind of long-haired working dog mixed in. Bear, as the shelter had named him, would have been a handsome fellow in his prime, but eating barely enough to stay alive, he was a good ten pounds underweight. Try as she might, Maddie had made little to no progress rehabilitating him.

She expected no different tonight as she carried Bear's bowl to the pen. So when she saw him standing at the gate, ears pricked and his full attention focused overhead, she gasped in surprise. "Hey, boy, what is it?"

The dog glanced her way, then toward the basement stairs. He let out a sharp bark—a sound she'd never heard from him in all the months he'd been here.

As she eased open the gate to his pen, the door at the top of the stairs creaked. "Ms. McNeill? The corn muffins are out. Can I—"

Barking wildly, Bear charged past Maddie, and the bowl of kibble went flying. She regained her footing in time to see the dog bounding up the steps. Next came the thud of two bodies colliding. From the bottom of the stairs, all Maddie could see was a fiercely wagging tail and the soles of Witt's gray wool socks.

What just happened here? Maddie knew from painful experience that she wasn't always the best judge of a man's character, but…could Bear have sensed something sinister about the handyman that she'd completely missed? Worried more for the dog's safety than her own, she seized the nearest thing to a weapon she could find—the heavy, enamel-coated metal bowl she used for custom-blending dog food—and crept up the stairs ready to strike.

Chapter Two

"Hey, hey! Take it easy, fella!" Witt clutched at the cheek fur of the black-and-tan beast that had him pinned to the floor. He turned his face away from the dog's hot breath and the slobbery tongue scraping across his cheeks.

Ranger?

"It *is* you! I can't believe it!"

Beyond the dog's shoulder, a mass of copper hair appeared at the top of the basement steps. Wielding a lethal-looking bowl, Maddie lunged for Ranger's collar. "Bear, stop! What's gotten into you?"

By now, Witt was laughing hysterically, while happy tears poured from his eyes. Arms wrapped around Ranger, who yipped like a puppy and hadn't quit licking his face, he tried to sit up. "This is my dog. I lost him over two years ago."

"What? Are you sure?"

"Not a doubt in the world." Taking a moment to catch his breath, Witt looked deep into the warm brown eyes of the dog who'd literally saved his life that snowy December day and then was hauled away by the animal control officer. "His name's Ranger, because when I found him, he—we were both—" His throat closed over the words he couldn't bring himself to say: *Lost. Lonely. Forsaken.*

Collapsing to the floor, Maddie sat back on her heels and shook her head. "I'm stunned. He'd been so depressed that I'd all but given up hope of ever seeing a spark of life in him. All this time, he was missing you."

As if to convince her he was fine now, Ranger whirled around to bestow a few doggy kisses on Maddie. Instantly, the dog was all over Witt again.

The clatter of a pot lid sounded behind them.

"Oh, no, the chili." Maddie scrambled to her feet and hurried to the stove.

Witt's hunger had been all but forgotten at the sight of his dog. As both his and Ranger's initial rush of elation ebbed, he could no longer stem his emotions. A sob burst from his chest. He buried his face in the dog's fur. "Ranger. My sweet boy Ranger."

Maddie's hand settled on his shoulder, tender and reassuring. "Are you okay?"

He looked up with a shaky but grateful smile. "Better than I've been in quite a while."

"Well, I rescued the chili, and we should eat the corn muffins while they're hot. Let me go down and get Bear's—excuse me, *Ranger's* food, and we can all have supper together."

By the time Maddie brought the meal to the table, Witt's appetite had returned with a vengeance. The not-too-spicy chili and corn muffins with butter and honey hit the spot.

Maddie had set Ranger's bowl on the floor near Witt's chair, and the dog chowed down with gusto. "Not so fast, boy," she cautioned with a laugh. "There's more where that came from."

Witt kept glancing at Ranger to reassure himself this was real. Countless nights he'd dreamed of reuniting with his dog, only to awaken and find himself alone. Worse were the nightmares when his brain conjured up all the horrible things that could have happened to Ranger. What if somebody with a mean streak had claimed him? What if he'd run away again and was fending for himself in unfriendly back alleys? What if he'd come to a cruel and untimely end?

"How?" he asked, awe in his tone. "How'd you come by him?"

She described how dogs typically came to her through local veterinarians and animal shelters. "My vet, who's also a good friend, happened upon him at one of the shelters. When he wouldn't eat and wouldn't make up to anyone, I became his last resort."

"Praise the Lord you could take him." Witt's voice broke. He shifted sideways to give Ranger another cuddle. "And that you hadn't given up."

"I don't give up easily," she stated. "And never on one of my dogs."

He met her firm gaze. "I got that about you right away."

Her glance wavered. She fiddled with her crumpled napkin. "At least I haven't so far. But unless—" She cut herself off with a head shake and pushed away from the table. "I should get started on these dishes."

"Let me help." Gathering his bowl, glass and flatware, Witt followed her to the sink.

She relieved him of the dishes as the sink filled with sudsy hot water. "I'll finish these later. The loft should be all warmed up by now, so I'll get you some supplies, and you can…" She hesitated, looking from him to Ranger, who was pressed against his knee. "You two won't stand for being parted again, will you?"

He chuckled. "I think not."

"Then you'd better take Ranger's bed and water bowl. His kennel's in the far corner of the basement, near the door to the backyard, if you don't mind running down to get them."

"Sure thing." Like there'd be any chance the old boy would be sleeping on the floor instead of snuggled on the bed next to Witt. How he'd missed draping his arm across that warm, furry body every night.

Ranger stayed right next to him as he made his way downstairs. He paused to greet a little white dog who appeared chipper and well-fed despite the healing skin lesions. Maddie McNeill clearly took good care of her animals. It wasn't her fault Ranger hadn't fared as well.

Overhead, the floor creaked beneath Maddie's footsteps. Witt glanced up, his attention caught by sagging joists, a sign of worse problems to come. Should he say anything? She might think he was only trolling for more business—maybe even trying to cheat her. He shuddered and clamped down on a repulsive memory.

But if one of those joists were to break, she could be hurt, or worse, and Witt couldn't live with that. Best case, she'd be saddled with some pretty expensive repairs, and she'd dropped more than a few hints today about her cash flow problem.

You're needed here, Witt.

Maybe so, but he couldn't work for nothing. He had to afford a place of his own—a place for him and Ranger now—because his two years at the transitional home would end June 1.

He clenched his jaw. He'd have to leave Ranger here until then, if Maddie didn't mind. Maybe she'd let him visit on the weekends. He could trade odd jobs around the place for Ranger's care.

"Finding everything okay?" she called from the top of the stairs.

"Yes, ma'am, be right up." Reaching into Ranger's pen, he grabbed the stainless-steel water bowl and a soft, fuzzy dog bed.

He emptied the bowl into the sink near the stairs, then headed up, careful not to be tripped by the dog glued to his side. It was as if Ranger wanted to make sure Witt never left his sight again. The feeling was mutual.

In the kitchen, Maddie had stuffed an oversize paper shopping bag with bedding and other supplies. "The snow's let up a bit, but it's pretty deep out there. Think you can make it across to the barn?"

"It's a straight shot. We'll do fine." As he set the dog bowl in the top of the bag, the floor creaked underfoot, and his thoughts returned to the structural problems he'd noticed in the basement. Tomorrow would be soon enough to approach Maddie about his trade-off idea. He'd do just about anything in his power to repay this woman for her kindness toward both him and his beloved dog.

Maddie watched from the mudroom door as Witt and his dog plodded through the drifts, the automatic yard lights illuminating their way through the deepening dark. What kind of a God thing was it that the very person she'd hired to repair the kennel roof should turn out to be the answer to her prayers about Bear?

Ranger, she corrected herself.

And half-hearted prayers at that, because most days she wasn't so certain God even listened.

She turned with a sigh. *If this is Your doing, Lord, then thanks. I'm glad for Witt and Ranger. Now, if You could show me how to keep this place going on a shoestring budget, please? Because these dogs need me.*

Truth be told, she needed *them*. Most of the dogs had been around since before her grandmother had passed away, including Joey, the white shepherd mix. He'd been Nana's favorite, and he'd known she'd died even before Maddie. One afternoon last fall, his mournful howls had alerted her as she'd been cleaning out dog runs. She'd gone to see what the matter was, only to find Nana collapsed on the kennel kitchen floor, her face serene but lifeless.

Distraught, Maddie had called 911, but the EMTs assured her there was nothing she could have done. The cause was later confirmed as hemorrhagic stroke, and death had followed almost instantly. It was small comfort.

She returned to the dishes she'd left soaking and made quick work of them. In the morning she'd have to figure out something to feed Witt for breakfast. Since she'd missed her chance to run to the market before the snow blew in, oatmeal would have to do.

The house phone rang, the landline a throwback to Nana's insistence on having reliable service out here where cell tower coverage could be spotty. The caller ID registered Frasier Family Veterinary Clinic. Must be Julia, calling to check on her. She carried the cordless handset to the table and sat down before answering.

"How'd the roof repair go?" her friend asked. "Did the guy finish before the storm?"

"Not quite, but he refused to quit till it was done. I fed him supper and let him have the barn loft for the night."

A pause. "Are you sure that's wise?"

"I was uneasy at first. But Witt's a dog lover, and the dogs definitely liked him. In fact—you'll never believe this—Bear's his dog."

Julia gasped. "You're kidding!"

Laughing, Maddie described the reunion and what Witt had told her about losing his dog two years ago. "If you could have seen them together—Julia, it about broke my heart. The man was weeping tears of joy."

"So Bear's name is really Ranger. Seems fitting. I always knew that dog had a story to tell." Julia sighed, and Maddie could picture her dark-haired friend's pensive gaze. "So you're sure this Witt person is an okay guy?"

Maddie snorted. Sometimes Julia could be a tad overprotective, though not without her reasons. "I'm fairly certain he isn't a serial killer."

"Not funny, Maddie. You know I worry about you."

"And I appreciate it. But most dog lovers I've met are good people, and I don't expect Witt to be the exception." She added another line to the sketch she'd begun while chatting with Julia. A pair of captivating eyes gazed back at her from the face of the man she'd met only hours ago.

"Just…promise me you'll be careful."

"I always am." It was true—Maddie's trust issues were too deeply ingrained, no thanks to her undependable mother, absent father, one particular lying creep of a boyfriend and, to top it off, the unscrupulous investment manager who'd cheated her grandparents out of most of their savings. Maddie would forever hold him and his company responsible for the heart attack that killed her grandfather and left Nana to scrape by until the strain took her life, too.

Julia broke her measured silence. "You know I love you, right?"

"Of course," Maddie said. "But you can't rescue me like one of those shelter dogs. I can take care of myself." If she didn't count a damaged kennel roof or the massive black hole of her financial situation.

Speaking of which… "I need to go. I still have to put Zoom lessons together for my Saturday online tutoring sessions." Fees from the students Frenchtown School District sent her way at least covered her grocery and utility bills.

If only she could figure out how to keep the donations coming in now that her astute and amiable grandmother no longer provided the public face for Eventide Dog Sanctuary.

By morning, the skies had cleared, painting the snow-covered ground with a shimmering blue-white sheen. Looking out the kitchen window, Maddie could barely discern where Witt and Ranger had carved a path in the snow on their way to the barn. She hoped they'd been comfortable enough in the loft. It hadn't been used, much less properly cleaned, since Nana had let their hired man go when she could no longer afford to pay him a decent wage.

Maddie had taken up as much of the slack as she

could, but it was never enough, and things had only gotten harder after Nana died. She braced her hands on the rim of the sink and let her chin drop. *Lord, are You paying attention? Because I don't know how much longer I can keep this up.*

She couldn't desert the dogs, though, for who else would take them in? Who else would love them enough to make their last days as comfortable and secure as humanly possible?

With a tired sigh, she started the coffee maker, then went downstairs to let Phoebe out for a brief run in a sheltered section of the backyard. She cleaned the kennel, fed the little dog and applied her meds. Phoebe's skin looked better every day. "You won't have to be quarantined down here much longer, baby girl, I promise."

Upstairs, she'd just donned her coat and boots when she glimpsed Witt and Ranger on their way down the outer stairs from the barn loft. Bracing herself, she stepped out into the cold. "Good morning. Did you sleep okay?"

"Like two bugs in a rug." Witt waved and smiled. Ranger still sported the same goofy grin he'd worn since reuniting with his master last evening.

It warmed Maddie's heart to see the dog so happy. "I'm on my way for morning rounds in the kennel. There's coffee in the kitchen if you want to help yourself."

"I can wait. Tell me how I can help you." He fell in step with her as she plodded through the drifts.

She resisted the impulse to put more distance between them. "Morning chores are mainly a repeat of last night—food and water, meds, cleaning out the runs—except a few of these pups will enjoy a romp in the snow. It's a process brushing the snow from their fur afterward, but it's worth it to let them have a little fun."

Inside, she pointed out which dogs were okay to release into the play yard, and Witt went around opening their doors. While she prepared breakfast bowls, he began cleaning the runs. A short time later, she called the dogs in from their romp. Handing Witt a wire whisk, she showed him how to brush away the icy clumps stuck to their legs and belly fur.

Once the dogs were back in their runs with food and fresh water, Maddie distributed meds, supplements and an extra pat or chin scratch. After a final check of each dog, she detoured to the barn to tend the horses. Witt insisted on mucking the stalls while she fed the mares and released them into their sunny paddock. With the animals taken care of, she invited Witt to the house for breakfast.

"Mugs are in the cupboard over the coffee maker," she said as she padded in sock feet to the pantry. "Oh, and Ranger's food is on the shelf at the foot of the stairs. He should have one scoop of dry kibble from the brown-and-red bag and also one of those chewable vitamin pills."

"On it." Witt headed down the basement steps.

After starting the oatmeal cooking, Maddie set the table and brought out milk, raisins and brown sugar. On her way across the kitchen, a floorboard creaked. The dip in the floor had become more noticeable lately, which didn't bode well. She probably ought to ask Witt about it, but fear of another huge expense made her cringe.

He returned with Ranger's bowl of kibble and set it

by the back door. While the dog ate, he poured himself a mug of coffee and leaned against the counter while Maddie stirred the oatmeal. "Smells good. That's not the instant stuff, is it?"

She laughed. "As my grandmother used to say, faster isn't always better."

"Wise woman. Is she still around?"

Maddie shook her head. "She passed away last fall."

"I'm sorry."

"Eventide was her life's mission, and this was her home." She circled her hand in a vague gesture meant to encompass the house and surrounding property. "My home, too, for most of my life. My father wasn't one to stick around, and my mother was pretty much useless, so my grandparents raised me." She didn't know why she was telling all this to a man she barely knew, but something about Witt put her at ease and the words tumbled out. "Gramps died about seven years ago, and when Nana's health began to fail last year, I came back to help. I never expected to lose her so soon, though. And now I—" Cutting herself off, she shook her head briskly to stem the welling tears.

When the man didn't immediately jump in with sympathy, she was grateful. It was embarrassing enough that she'd so freely poured out her life story—the high points anyway, the parts she could afford to recall without risking a complete meltdown.

"Oatmeal's done," she declared with a sniff. "Have a seat and I'll serve it up."

Witt sensed his host was treading through difficult emotional territory this morning, and he wished he knew how to respond. He also knew from experience that sometimes there were no words. Sometimes you just had to sit with your feelings and let them quietly speak their truth.

He'd noticed last night that Maddie hadn't paused to say grace over their supper. A ceramic cross and a framed needlework prayer hung over the kitchen table—*Come, Lord Jesus, be our guest. Let these gifts to us be blessed.* Apparently she'd grown up in a faith-filled home. Perhaps she'd been too distracted by the commotion over his reunion with Ranger.

Once she'd filled their bowls and took her seat, he nodded toward the prayer on the wall. "That's one of my favorites."

She glanced up, a sad smile curling her lips. "It was my grandmother's favorite, too. Ever since I was a little girl, we'd repeat it together before meals. I... I've kind of fallen out of the habit since she's gone."

Now Witt felt bad for reminding her. "How about I just offer a brief word of thanks?"

"Yes. Please." She bowed her head.

When he finished, she said a quiet thank-you, then passed him the oatmeal toppings and milk. The hot and hearty breakfast soon filled the nooks and crannies of his empty stomach.

Again, he offered to help with the dishes, but she said she'd do them later. "The weatherman says it'll warm up quickly today, so it shouldn't be long before we can clear the lane enough to get your truck out. By then, the plows should have the main roads passable."

"No hurry," Witt said, weighing his next words. "Matter of fact, I wanted to approach you with an idea."

On her way to the pantry, she glanced over her shoulder with a questioning look. Then an ominous crack sounded beneath her next step. She froze, her gaze locked on his. "That didn't sound good."

"Maybe move to one side," he said, picturing the weak joists he'd observed last night. "Carefully."

She took one giant step to her left, then breathed a relieved sigh. "This floor's been a worry for a while now, but I've been too scared to find out what it would cost to fix."

"That's kind of what I wanted to talk to you about. See, this place where I'm living right now doesn't allow pets, so I've been trying to figure out what to do with Ranger." He shared his thoughts about leaving the dog with Maddie until he could find another place and re-paying her with whatever repairs she might need.

"I'd be happy for Ranger to stay with me as long as necessary, but I seriously doubt he's going to be satisfied with such an arrangement." Stepping cautiously, she continued to the pantry with the canister of brown sugar. "Besides, it seems like a lopsided trade-off, considering all the work I obviously need done around here."

She wasn't wrong—about Ranger or about the work needed. The little Witt had seen of Maddie's house and outbuildings suggested the place could benefit from a lot more attention than he could give it in a few week-ends. She had no business trying to manage all this single-handedly, but she struck him as a woman too stubborn to admit it.

Arms folded, she crossed to the sink and stared out the window. "The unavoidable fact of the matter is that I need help."

So…not too stubborn after all. He decided to keep his mouth shut and let her talk.

She pivoted to face him. "You need a place to live that allows dogs. I need a maintenance person and kennel assistant. I can't afford to pay much, but I can offer you the barn loft and three meals a day. And you could still keep working for Happy's Helpers."

Witt's jaw dropped. "Are you sure about this? Because you barely know a thing about me, and—"

"I know you love dogs, and I saw yesterday how long and hard you'll work to finish a job." She hesitated, the tiniest flicker of doubt making her glance away briefly. Then she hiked her chin. "Please. Say yes before I realize what an absurd idea this is and change my mind."

Kneeling, he called his dog over and pressed Ranger's face between his hands. "What do you think, boy? Should we accept this lady's kind offer before she comes to her senses?"

Ranger yipped and licked Witt's nose.

"I'll take that as a yes." He stood and extended his right hand to Maddie. "You're an answer to my prayers, Ms. McNeill. In more ways than you can possibly imagine."

Eventually he'd have to tell her more about himself—not the worst of which was his full name, Angus Nathaniel Wittenbauer. As the first and only child of his well-meaning parents, he'd been saddled with the first names of both his grandfathers. Long before reaching school age, though, he'd been dubbed simply Witt.

Yes, giving his name would be the easy part. He'd rather hide forever the shame he couldn't quite release, the grim choices that had cost him his home and family…the lonely, despairing years on the street.

But for now, at least, he had a decent job, he had his dog back, and they'd just been given a home.

God was good. So very, very good.

Chapter Three

Witt tucked a pair of sneakers into the duffel bag along with the rest of his meager possessions. This morning, Monday, he'd be moving to Maddie McNeill's barn loft.

Carl, his counselor, ambled into the room. "How's the packing going?"

"All done." He zipped up the bag. "I'm as ready as I'll ever be."

Carl sank onto the bed next to the duffel. "I'm real proud of how far you've come over the past couple of years. We'll miss you around here, though. You've been a strong example and mentor for the newer guys."

Until that moment, Witt hadn't realized how much he'd miss not only the companionship of his housemates but Carl's guidance and support. Was he *really* ready for this? When his choices had destroyed so many lives, including his own, what made him deserving of another chance? What if he totally blew it?

What if he let Maddie and those dogs down?

"Stop," Carl quietly commanded. "I can guess what's going through your head. But God is stronger than your fear. Stop doubting His power to create your new life, and even more, to sustain it."

"It isn't God I doubt. It's me." Witt paced to the door and back. He didn't have to leave the home quite yet—he had a few more weeks until his time would be up here.

But he wouldn't have Ranger with him, and come June 1, he'd be facing the same dilemma all over again.

Bouncing up from the bed, Carl slung the duffel strap over his shoulder. "Let's go. I'll walk you out to your truck."

Somehow, his counselor's certainty fed his, and at the moment, he trusted the man more than he did himself. He followed Carl down the hall and through the living room, where several of his housemates had lined up to shake his hand and wish him well.

"Come back and see us when you can."

"You can do this, man. We're all pulling for you."

"Prayers, brother. God's got this."

Eyes welling, he could barely respond to each good-bye. Nods and heartfelt smiles would have to suffice.

At the truck, Carl shoved the duffel through the passenger-side door, then threw his arms around Witt in a bear hug. "You know you can call me anytime, day or night. And you'd better stay in touch and let me know how you're doing."

"I will. Thanks, Carl…for everything."

Before he completely lost it, he marched around the battered old truck and climbed behind the wheel. With a wave and two quick taps on the horn, he drove away. It helped to remember he'd be seeing Ranger again shortly.

When he turned in at the sign for Eventide Dog Sanctuary, his heart sped up. The sun-dappled lane was muddy from melting snow, and though daytime highs since Saturday had crept into the fifties, small drifts lingered anywhere the sun didn't reach.

As he neared the house, he glimpsed Maddie with several dogs in the fenced yard outside the kennel. Most were sniffing or exploring or stretched out to bask in the sunshine, except for one familiar black-and-tan mutt who sat by the gate looking forlorn.

Then suddenly the dog's ears perked up. As Witt stepped from the truck, Ranger backed up for a running start and cleared the fence in a flying leap. Seconds later, he braced his muddy paws on Witt's chest while dancing on his back legs and yipping like a puppy.

Laughing, he fought to keep his balance. "Easy, fella, I told you I'd be back!"

Maddie came through the gate, clomping through puddles in her knee-high muck boots. "I tried to tell him, too," she said, "but seeing is believing. Need any help moving your things up to the loft?"

"There's not that much. I travel light."

"Okay, then. Come to the house after you settle in. I'll have lunch ready, and afterward we can take care of the formalities."

He cringed inwardly. Naturally, she'd want some kind of contract spelling out the terms of their arrangement, which would likely mean supplying more background information. How would she react to learning he was recovering from alcoholism and homelessness? He should have been up front from the moment she'd made her offer.

It was too late now. He'd have to trust that Maddie McNeill would show as much compassion for him as she did for those dogs whose lives she'd blessed.

He grabbed his duffel from the truck, and Ranger

traipsed after him upstairs to the loft. He made the dog wait on the landing while he found an old towel to clean the mud off his paws, then an hour later did so again before allowing Ranger through Maddie's back door.

"Oh, don't worry about it," she said as she stirred something on the stove. "That's what mops are for."

"Thanks, but I'd rather not cause you extra trouble on my first day here." Witt kicked off his work boots and left them in the mudroom. Stepping into the kitchen, he glanced toward the dip in the floor, where one of the kitchen chairs now stood guard. "You've been avoiding the trouble spot, I see. I'll get busy on those joists first thing."

A few minutes later, they lunched on tomato soup and grilled cheese sandwiches. "I'm not a fancy cook," Maddie apologized. "With everything else on my plate—pardon the pun—when it comes to meals, I keep things simple."

"Simple is fine." He slurped a spoonful of soup. "Better than fine."

She swallowed a bite of sandwich. "I noticed you carried up just the one piece of luggage. Did you leave the rest behind for now? I mean, I'd understand if you wanted to do this on a trial basis until we see how it goes."

"No, I'm in this for keeps—that is, as long as the arrangement's working for you." He cleared his throat and took a sip of water. Time for honesty. "The truth is, everything I own is in that duffel. I—I'm getting back on my feet after—after—" Now that it came right down to it, he couldn't push the words out.

Maddie stiffened and leaned away, her eyes wary. "Are you an ex-con? Because if you are—"

"No, no, nothing like that." He'd been spared the fate of his former employer and several coworkers. But he hadn't been spared the guilt by association, or the repercussions. He took a deep breath and plunged on. "I lost my job several years back. I was angry and depressed and drank so much that my wife finally kicked me out. I ended up living on the streets. Most days I prayed I'd wake up dead."

"Oh, Witt." The compassion in her tone had returned.

Ranger crept closer and rested his chin on Witt's thigh. He wove his fingers through the dog's fur. "Then this fella wandered into my life and gave me something to live for. He's the whole reason—well, him and a lot of help from the Lord—that I'm alive today."

"But how'd you get separated?"

He told her how he'd gotten sick that winter two years ago while he and Ranger were living in a box under an overpass. What started as a simple cold had worsened into pneumonia, and he'd been seriously ill. He vaguely recalled Ranger howling like a banshee, which alerted Witt's neighbors until one of them flagged down a police car and told them to send an ambulance.

"Ranger wouldn't have left my side, except of course they wouldn't let him into the ambulance with me. Animal Control had to come and forcibly restrain him."

"And you never saw him again until he came charging up my basement steps." Laughing softly, Maddie shook her head. "What happened after you recovered? You've obviously been working on a fresh start."

"I went into rehab and then was accepted into a transitional residence program for recovering homeless men. My counselor helped me get my head on straight and connected me with some job leads. I rediscovered how much I used to enjoy working with my hands, and that's how I ended up with Happy's Helpers."

"So you weren't always a handyman? What did you do before?"

His throat closed. He glanced away. "Sorry, that's a part of my life I'm trying to forget."

It wasn't that Maddie wanted to press Witt for details he wasn't comfortable talking about, but shouldn't she know at least something about his previous work experience? For that matter, she still didn't know his full name.

You are a case, Maddie McNeill, taking on a one-named stranger with a sketchy past and letting him move into your barn. What's gotten into you?

She decided to give them both a break from the third degree and excused herself to clear the table. When she looked out the window over the sink, she glimpsed Julia's SUV pulling up next to the kennel. She'd all but forgotten Julia would be out this afternoon to give a few of the dogs their six-month checkups and update any vaccinations that were due.

Her stomach plummeted. Did she have enough money in the checking account to cover today's vet bill? Julia donated her services but had to recoup a portion of her costs for meds and vaccines.

"Everything okay?" Witt asked as he brought his dishes to the counter.

"I forgot an appointment." She nodded toward the window. "My vet is here."

"Anything I can do to help?"

"No, thanks. Maybe you could start working on my sagging floor?"

"I'll get my tools. Mind if I take another look at the scrap wood in the barn?"

"Take anything you can use." She followed him to the mudroom and pulled on her muck boots and sweater. "I'll be in the kennel if you need anything."

When she stepped inside the kennel, Julia had just brought out Rocky. Even at nine years old and missing a foreleg, the tan-and-white beagle-boxer mix could be a handful.

"Just in time," Julia said as she tried to keep the squirming Rocky from escaping. "This little guy's due for Bordetella and canine influenza."

"Oh joy," Maddie deadpanned. When it came to shots, Rocky was worse than a kid at the pediatrician's. Not that she knew firsthand what that was like. She'd always wanted children, but some things weren't meant to be. Besides the fact that she'd long ago decided she was through with relationships, her biological clock was striking midnight.

"That pickup by the barn," Julia began as she lifted Rocky onto the folding exam table she used for the smaller dogs. "Your handyman didn't stay all weekend, did he?"

Maddie huffed. Her friend would find out sooner or later. "Actually, he's living here now. I let him have the barn loft."

"You *what*?" Julia's jaw dropped. Taking advantage of her inattention, Rocky tried to make a break.

"Close your mouth," Maddie said as she corralled the feisty pup. "It's a mutually beneficial arrangement. Where he was living doesn't allow pets. I could use an extra hand around here, so I suggested a trade-off and he accepted." To say anything more about Witt's history would only stoke her friend's worries.

With a scowl, Julia returned her focus to the dog and thankfully didn't ask more questions about Maddie's new tenant.

A few nips, yips and toenail scratches later, they finished with Rocky. Next, Julia examined Joey, the white German shepherd mix. His arthritis seemed worse, so she suggested Maddie increase his anti-inflammatory dosage slightly. "Easy walks will help keep his joints working. Are you still giving him the glucosamine supplements?"

Looking into the dog's trusting eyes, Maddie stroked his head. "I am, but…is there anything less expensive we could try?"

Julia cast her a sympathetic smile. "Let me see if I can find you some discounts."

"Thanks. Money's tight right now." Maddie blew out a sharp sigh. "I'll never be the fundraiser my grandmother was."

She returned Joey to his run while Julia brought out the next dog. After they'd attended to two more, Julia checked her list. "That just leaves Phoebe."

"She's looking much better. I'm hoping you'll say it's okay to start socializing her."

As they started across to the house, Witt exited the barn with an armload of two-by-fours, Ranger trotting alongside. He nodded a greeting.

"So that's Bear's—I mean Ranger's 'dad'?" Julia pursed her lips. "I hope you weren't taken in by his good looks."

"Hush. He'll hear you." Maddie's face heated. She

slowed her pace to give Witt time to go inside and head down to work on the floor joists.

Julia groaned. "I'm sorry. I shouldn't be on your case about this guy. You're a smart woman and I should trust your judgment."

"Yes, I am, and yes, you should." Although sometimes Maddie wasn't so sure, herself. Shaking her head, she continued to the back door. "He's doing some repairs in the basement, so don't you dare say anything embarrassing when we go down to see Phoebe."

"*Moi?* I wouldn't dream of it."

"Hmm. Aren't you the same person who not two months ago told off the guy behind the Five on Black restaurant counter because you didn't like the way he was looking at you?"

"Well, he…he had a weird smile." Julia shivered. "He made me nervous."

Holding the door for her friend, Maddie rolled her eyes. "He was stifling a laugh because of how you pronounced *chimichurri.*"

"So I'm not good with languages. That was just rude."

Downstairs, Witt had his metal tape measure out and appeared to be deep in thought. Maddie hoped his grimace didn't mean more bad news. She had to laugh, though, at the sight of Ranger sitting next to Witt's leg and staring up at the ceiling with the same intensity as his master.

Witt turned, his frown morphing into a smile. "My 'assistant' and I were just strategizing. I'll need to pick up a couple of things, but the cost should be minimal."

"That's good." Because even minimal would be pushing Maddie's limits these days.

Julia stepped up beside her and thrust out a hand. "Hello, I'm Julia Frasier, Maddie's vet. I couldn't believe it when she told me about you and Bear—I mean Ranger."

Witt accepted her handshake. "Happiest day of my life. Second happiest was Ms. McNeill's offer of a place for us to live. God's blessed me twice in a matter of days."

"The Lord surely works in mysterious ways." Julia arched a brow. "By the way, I'm also Maddie's very best friend, and we keep an eye out for each other. Regularly. Every day, practically."

So much for not saying anything embarrassing. "I'm sure you have other patients to see this afternoon, don't you, Julia?" Maddie gave her friend a pointed look. "Maybe you should check Phoebe now."

"Right. I'm sure I'll be seeing you around, Witt."

A few minutes later, Julia pronounced Phoebe fully recovered and ready to be around other dogs. Maddie followed her upstairs to the kitchen. "I'm a little low on funds until I get my tutoring check. Can I pay you after the first of the month?"

"Of course, no rush." With an apologetic frown, Julia drew her into a quick hug. "Witt does seem like a nice guy. It's just that I remember what you went through after Garrett, and I never want to see your heart stomped on like that again."

"In that regard, you have nothing to worry about, because I have permanently renounced all future romantic entanglements."

"That isn't what I meant, and you know it. You deserve to be happy. Truly happy, with a decent man who'll treat you right."

"So do you, Jules. But as we both have learned from painful experience, good men are hard to find."

"Indeed they are."

Once Julia had left, Maddie pulled out a kitchen chair and collapsed into it. Her situation seemed dismal enough without being reminded of the man who'd strung her along for so many years with promises of marriage only to discover he already had a wife and three kids. She'd vowed then that no man would ever be allowed close enough to hurt or deceive her again.

No human, anyway. There was no keeping a lock on her heart where the dogs were concerned. She loved them all and mourned each inevitable loss more keenly than the one before.

The creaking basement steps drew her attention. She straightened and pasted on a smile as Witt and Ranger appeared in the doorway.

But not quickly enough, judging from the concerned look on Witt's face. "If you're still worried about repair costs, the fix I'm planning won't be expensive at all. I just need a couple of ten-foot four-by-fours to brace the weak joists and..."

As he described what he had in mind, Maddie could only smile and nod. Nana might have understood the carpentry terms—Grandpa would have done the repairs himself—but Maddie knew zilch about this kind of stuff.

When Witt stopped talking and wrinkled his brow, she realized her eyes must have glazed over. "Sorry, that's all over my head."

"Ms. McNeill—"

"Just Maddie, please."

"Maddie." His frown deepened. "Are you all right?"

No, not in the least, she wanted to say. But there was no possible way she could explain. Every wound, every fear, every regret she'd amassed in her forty-six years clung and clawed and choked her until some days she could barely breathe.

"I'm fine. A busy day, that's all." She stood tiredly and hiked her chin. "I need to make space for Phoebe in the kennel, and then I have to be online at four o'clock for a tutoring session. So buy whatever you need for the repairs, and I'll reimburse you." *Eventually.*

Before he could question her further, she hurried out.

He didn't believe her. Not one single word. Something was eating at Maddie, and Witt suspected it involved a whole lot more than a cash flow problem. The haunted look in her eyes a few moments ago wasn't so different from what he'd often seen in his own face every time he glimpsed himself in a reflective surface.

Maybe someday she'd trust him enough to be honest with him.

"Wanna go for a ride, Ranger? I've come a long way since we parted company. I have my own truck now." And a meager bank account and even a low-limit credit card, thanks to Carl's putting in a good word for him with the bank manager. There wasn't much a person could do these days without credit.

On his way home—the very word brought a catch to his heart—he glimpsed Maddie riding one of the horses across a pasture. Joey, the white German shepherd, ambled alongside. Witt slowed, rolled down his window and tipped his cap.

She waved and reined the Palomino—named Sunny, as he recalled—toward the fence. "My tutoring student canceled, so I decided to go for a ride. Did you find everything you needed to fix the floor?"

Motioning with his thumb toward the pickup bed, he nodded. "I'll have it shored up by suppertime."

"That *shore* sounds good to me," she said with a grin.

He laughed and continued to the house. It was nice to see Maddie smiling, something he guessed she didn't do nearly often enough. A horseback ride on a pleasant Montana afternoon must have been just what she needed.

Later, as he finished in the basement, the clatter of pots and pans told him she'd started supper. He hefted his toolbox and an armful of wood scraps and headed upstairs. "All done. How's it looking from up here?"

Turning from the stove, she cast her gaze across the section of floor where the dip used to be. She nodded approvingly. "Except for the warped flooring, you'd never know there'd been a problem."

Witt frowned at the misshapen black-and-white checkerboard tiles. "I'll see what I can do about those tomorrow. I should also work on a more permanent fix for the kennel roof. And I noticed a tricky doorknob—"

"Slow down," she said with a slightly panicked laugh. "It's okay to pace yourself. Anyway, you need to leave time for your handyman job, and I, um…" Her glance skittered sideways.

Back to the money issue, obviously. "I get it, no hurry. But you've been so kind to me—" Ranger nosed his hand "—to both me and my dog—and I want to repay that kindness as best I can."

"You're already doing so." While stirring something on the stove, she motioned distractedly toward the back door. "For now, you should finish up and get ready for supper."

He took a couple of steps, then paused. "If it makes you more comfortable, I'm happy to take my meals up to the loft. Our arrangement shouldn't mean an intrusion on your privacy."

Her shoulders rose and fell in a long, slow breath. Without looking at him, she murmured, "We'll see how it goes."

Nodding to himself, Witt strode out through the mudroom. Again, he recognized something in Maddie evocative of his own experience. There were times in his life when he'd chosen to be alone. But the hopelessness, the utter desolation, of true loneliness? That was altogether different.

It was clear that Maddie's veterinary friend was someone she relied on and who tenaciously looked out for her. Even so, something told him Maddie had pushed everyone else away for so long that loneliness had become second nature, and now she wrestled with the conundrum of letting in someone new.

For reasons he couldn't explain, he wanted it to be him.

Chapter Four

Fists planted against her hips, Maddie eyed the newly replaced kitchen floor tiles. Ensconced in the study most of the afternoon while tutoring her online students, she hadn't heard a thing. Julia would certainly have a few choice words about her sudden willingness to trust a relative stranger with the run of the place.

But Witt had certainly proven both his worth and his honesty since moving to the sanctuary exactly one week ago. When he wasn't out on a Happy's Helpers call, he'd found time to fix a leaky faucet, replace a cracked windowpane, clean out gutters… Maddie had lost count of all the minor repairs he'd completed. So far, at least, nothing had been too costly.

Hearing sounds from the mudroom, she glimpsed Witt through the door glass. With a smile, she motioned him inside.

He scraped his boots across the mat before stepping into the kitchen. "How's the floor look?"

"As good as new." She hesitated to ask, but… "How much do I owe you for the tiles?"

"Not a thing. I asked around and found another Happy's Helpers guy who's putting in a new floor for a client. They were pulling up almost these exact same tiles, so I rescued several of the better ones from the dumpster. Pretty good match, huh?"

"A *very* good match. Wow. Thank you."

"Oh, here's your mail." Witt handed her the bundle. "I heard the postman's truck as I was putting my tools away, so I walked down to the box."

"You didn't have to do that." Maddie usually drove to the mailbox in the rusty golf cart Nana had bought thirdhand years ago.

"No problem. Needed to stretch my legs anyway, and Ranger was ready for a romp." He gave the dog's head a pat. As always, the scruffy animal was glued to Witt's side.

As Maddie riffled through the mail, a business envelope drew her attention. It bore the logo of a Missoula pet supply store that supported Eventide both financially and with gifts in kind. Hopeful the envelope contained a sizable check, she tore open the flap.

But when she read the enclosed letter, printed on official company stationery, her heart sank. "No. Oh, no, no, no."

Witt sidled closer. "Bad news?"

She thrust the page at him, then sank into the nearest chair and dropped her head into her hands.

Behind her, he read the words: ...*re-evaluating the direction of our charitable giving...decision has been made to discontinue contributions to Eventide Dog Sanctuary...our sincere regrets*...

"Oh, Maddie, I'm so sorry." He plopped into a chair.

"This is my fault. Nana would never have let this

happen." She sniffed and sat back, her gaze sweeping the ceiling as if she'd find answers there.

Lips pursed, Witt massaged his jaw. "Maybe if you called them, spoke to someone directly—"

"That's just it. I'm terrible at public relations—especially asking for money." A sob caught in her throat. "All I want is to live a quiet life and take care of my dogs. I don't have it in me to give fundraising speeches or sweet-talk business owners into writing big checks."

"Is that what your grandmother did?"

"Yes, but much more gracefully than I made it sound." She blew out a sharp sigh. "Nana was inspiring. She knew how to invite others into her vision for Eventide so that they wanted to contribute."

Ranger whined and rested his chin on Witt's knee. He gave the dog a loving scratch behind the ears. "Yeah, boy, I know. We'll have to think of something."

His choice of words caught her attention. "We?"

He blinked. "Sorry, didn't mean to presume. It's just… I've seen firsthand the difference you're making in these dogs' lives." Glancing away, he murmured, "Mine, too."

A look in his eye, a shift in his posture, a word softly spoken…he hid it well most of the time, but there were moments when Witt's brokenness revealed itself in a way that stabbed Maddie's heart. She could only wonder about the tragic turn of events that had once nearly destroyed this good man.

And here she sat fretting over the loss of one Eventide supporter. She had a brain and a voice. If she cared for her dogs as much as she claimed to, certainly she could step out of her comfort zone now and then to keep donations coming in—even if the mere thought made her stomach cramp.

She steeled her spine. "You're right, Witt—we'll think of something. I don't know what yet, but we can't let these dogs down."

His smile returned. "That's the spirit. Anything I can do to help, you only have to ask."

"I will. And Witt?" She waited for him to meet her gaze. "You're making a difference in my life, too."

"That's kind of you to say." With a rough clear of his throat, he stood. "I'd best get on with chores. Those kennel pups will be wanting their supper pretty soon."

"I'll be out as soon as I finish with the mail."

When he and Ranger had gone, she perused the usual assortment of ads and junk mail, then tossed most of it in the recycling bin. Elk Valley was too small to have its own recycling service, but once a month or so, she toted her accumulation to a drop-off in Missoula.

She deposited the rest of the mail on her desk in the study, then opened her sketch pad. After that first day, when she'd attempted to capture Witt's expressive eyes on a piece of scratch paper, she'd hoped to improve on her efforts. She laid the original sketch next to the new one. Incredible that in only a week's time, she discerned the subtle changes in him.

Turning to another page, she examined her first drawing of Ranger, the drooping head and listless eyes so different from the dog he was today. It was definitely time for a new portrait. She'd start tonight.

Later that evening, Witt propped up his pillows, turned on the bedside lamp and made room for Ranger alongside him on top of the quilt. He'd planned to do some reading, but he couldn't get Maddie off his mind. As they'd taken care of kennel chores and then had supper together, she'd said nothing more about the letter. He could tell she was scared, though, and more worried about the future of Eventide Dog Sanctuary than she dared admit.

He couldn't help worrying, too. If Eventide failed, it would break Maddie's heart. And not only would all the animals be displaced but so would he. With Ranger by his side again, not to mention twenty-plus other dogs and a couple of horses to shower with affection, this was his home now. He couldn't lose it. Not again.

Heaving a sigh, he opened the mystery novel he'd borrowed from Maddie's bookshelf a few days ago. He'd been marking his place with a folded piece of scrap paper Maddie must have left between the pages. He hadn't paid much attention to the scrap, but now, out of idle curiosity, he took a closer look. On the outside, it appeared nothing more than an old grocery list—milk, eggs, soup, crackers...

But when he spread open the paper and flipped it over, the pencil sketch of a dog looked back at him. With one eye squinting, tongue hanging out and ears cocked, there was no mistaking the subject—Rocky, the mischievous three-legged beagle mix from the kennel. In a few deft strokes, the artist had captured the dog's sassy expression perfectly.

He flipped back to the shopping list. The handwriting looked like Maddie's. Was the sketch hers, too? If so, she had real talent, and he was eager to ask her about it.

Finding something else to use as a bookmark, he tucked the sketch into the pocket of the flannel shirt he'd laid out for tomorrow. Then, as best he could, he set his mind to unraveling the clues in the mystery novel.

The next morning, he was already at work in the kennel when Maddie came out. Yawning, she joined him in the kitchen, where he was measuring kibble into bowls. "You don't have to do *everything* around here, Witt. Otherwise, I'll start thinking I'm irrelevant."

"Never in a million years." He shook out two of Joey's joint supplement chews and placed them atop the dog's food.

Later, with the dogs sniffing around or chasing each other in the play yard, Witt pulled the folded scrap of paper from his pocket and nonchalantly handed it to Maddie. "Found this in the book I borrowed. Thought it might be important."

"An old shopping list?" She scoffed. "Hardly."

He stopped her before she could wad it up to discard. "Actually, I was referring to what's inside."

Casting a frown his way, she unfolded the paper. A small gasp escaped. "Oh, this. I'd forgotten all about it." With a crooked grin, she added, "That Rocky's such a character."

"And you're quite the artist."

"Oh, please. Doodling is just a habit I fall back on when I need to de-stress." Turning her attention to the dogs, she called, "Joey, be gentle with Phoebe. You're a lot bigger than she is."

He wasn't going to let her shut down the topic so easily. "That sketch hardly qualifies as a doodle. Are there more?"

"A few." Her indifferent shrug barely disguised the tension across her shoulders. She strode over to where one of the dogs was rolling in something. "Keep it up, Boots, and you'll earn yourself a bath this afternoon."

The toothless black-and-tan sheltie with four white paws immediately got up and sauntered off.

"I'd like to see them," Witt called across the yard.

"See what?"

"Your drawings."

"I told you, they're just doodles." She clapped her hands. "Come on, gang, time for naps."

Stubborn woman. Was she merely being modest, or was there another reason she didn't want to share her art?

As they returned the dogs to their runs, Witt got a handyman call and needed to head into Missoula. Ranger already looked forward to riding shotgun on these trips and was good about waiting for him in the pickup or, if it was an outdoor job, staying close by but out of the way.

This job involved repairing and staining a backyard deck, which likely meant two or three workdays. And a nice little check upon completion. Parking in the driveway of the attractive split-level home, Witt did his usual gut check. While he'd come to love working for Happy's Helpers, he'd had to get past the fact that most of his clients enjoyed the lifestyle he'd forfeited all those years ago—and not merely the well-appointed suburban home, professionally landscaped lawn and a couple of shiny late-model cars in the driveway. Those were merely the outward symbols of success.

For Witt, the real loss had been the love and respect of his wife, his children, his friends. He'd burned too many bridges to ever hope for their forgiveness. Now, all he could do was lean into God's mercy and continue rebuilding some semblance of respect for himself.

Next question—ring the front doorbell, or go around back? He gave Ranger a pat. "Better stay here till I get the lay of the land."

He'd just stepped from the pickup when a tall, silver-haired man came down the front steps. "You must be Witt. Hi, I'm David Caldwell."

"Yes, sir, I understand you need some deck work." He gestured up the driveway. "Around back?"

Nodding, Mr. Caldwell glanced in the pickup window. "Brought a helper, I see. Your dog's welcome to come along."

Witt liked the guy already. He opened the passenger door for Ranger, then hefted his toolbox from the pickup bed and followed the man up the driveway.

At the rear of the house, an aging wooden deck jutted out on four-foot support posts. A slender woman, her long dark hair in a ponytail, was moving potted plants off the deck. Mr. Caldwell introduced her as his wife, Alicia. She looked his way with a warm smile. "Hello. I'm glad you were available so quickly. Our son used to take care of the yearly maintenance, but he's living in Texas now."

A quick inspection proved quality workmanship and regular upkeep. However, winter had taken a toll on the steps and a few of the boards. One of the support posts had gotten a little wobbly, too. After taking measurements and jotting some notes, Witt headed to the builders' supply. Returning with wood, deck screws and two cans of water-repellent stain, he set to work.

It was turning into a warm spring day, and by noon he was peeling off his flannel shirt and mopping his brow with the sleeve of his gray T-shirt. About that time, the Caldwells carried out trays of sandwiches, chips and canned drinks.

"Thought you might be ready for some lunch." Mrs. Caldwell arranged the food on the glass-top patio table they'd moved under a shade tree.

In the meantime, her husband refreshed the water bowl Witt had brought for Ranger. "Feel free to wash up in the house. The powder room is just off the kitchen."

"Thanks. This is real nice of you." Witt kicked off his work boots and left them by the door as he went inside.

When he returned, Mr. Caldwell was fawning over Ranger, and the dog was eating up the attention. Over lunch, the Caldwells asked how Ranger had come into Witt's life. He couldn't give a full answer without admitting his former homelessness, but their kindness quickly put him at ease, and the more he talked, the less inclined he was to gloss over that part of the story.

The part he loved telling most was how he'd been reunited with Ranger when Maddie called him out for a job at her dog sanctuary, and then the Caldwells wanted to hear all about that.

"She's doing a wonderful thing for those dogs," he said, then remembered he'd rescued the sketch of Rocky from the trash can after they'd finished in the kennel that morning. He reached for his flannel shirt and plucked the scrap of paper from the pocket. After smoothing it out on the table, he showed the sketch to Mrs. Caldwell. "Here's a drawing Maddie did of one of the pups."

"What a cutie! Look, David. Wouldn't it be fun to have an artist at the fair who could do on-the-spot drawings of people's pets?" She turned to Witt. "Our church hosts an annual Memorial Day arts and crafts event. I realize it's last-minute, but do you think she'd be interested?"

"I don't know…" He couldn't forget Maddie's evasiveness about the sketch.

"Would you ask her, though? Animal lovers can be big spenders when it comes to their fur babies. Our vendors keep seventy-five percent of their sales, and it's just a hundred dollars to rent a booth."

His ears had perked up at the mention of the vendors' percentage, but the cost of the booth would be a deal breaker. "Her finances are kind of tight right now. The booth rental would be a stretch." And that didn't count persuading her to take the risk and share her talent.

Mrs. Caldwell pulled her lower lip between her teeth. "As the committee chair, I have some leeway about discounting or even waiving the booth fee. Please, will you at least ask her? I'm sure we can work something out."

All he could do was try. And this opportunity did seem like yet another answered prayer. *Lord, if this is how You want to help Maddie keep caring for those dogs, You'll have to help me convince her.*

"No! Absolutely, positively no!" Cast-iron skillet in hand, Maddie stomped to the pantry. Good thing Witt had already fixed the floor, or she might have ended up in the basement with a broken leg—or worse. At the moment, she was seriously considering using the skillet on Witt's thick head.

"Come on, Maddie, it's a chance to raise a little money for the dogs. Would you at least look at the brochure Mrs. Caldwell gave me?"

She set the skillet on a shelf, then waved away the shiny trifold he was brandishing and stepped around him. "You are entirely too presumptuous. And too nosy. And too…a whole lot of other words I'm too much of a lady to say." At the sink, she pulled the stopper and watched the dishwater drain out. To herself, she muttered, "Give the man an inch and he takes a mile."

Behind her, he'd gone silent except for his annoyed breaths. Well, let him be annoyed. He had no right butting into her business. Maybe if she ignored him long enough, he'd take the hint and leave.

"I'm not leaving till you sit down and listen to me, Maddie McNeill."

A low growl rumbling in her throat, she slowly turned to face him. "All right, *Angus*," she began, having quickly learned how the use of his given name raised his hackles, "say your piece if you must. But it won't change my mind."

He disappointed her with barely a flinch, then waited for her to return to her chair before taking his seat. Ranger dropped to his haunches beside Witt and glared at Maddie with the same intensity as his master.

Great. Two against one.

Fingers laced in her lap, she sat back and challenged the meddlesome handyman with a direct gaze of her own.

Releasing a weary sigh, he closed his eyes and dipped his chin as if praying. He ought to pray she wouldn't evict him over this. When he looked up again, his expression had softened. "Maddie, I just want to help. If you can dash off such a realistic sketch of Rocky on a tiny scrap of paper, imagine what others would be willing to pay for a professional drawing of their pets. Mrs. Caldwell thinks you could easily ask twenty dollars apiece, fifteen of which is yours to keep. Even if you had only ten customers—and she expects you'd have a lot more takers—that's an easy hundred and fifty dollars. Tell me it wouldn't be worth it."

"Easy? *Easy?*" Her stomach heaved at the very thought. "I can't put myself out there like that. It's—it's too much pressure. And I'm certainly no professional. What if I…"

"Fail? Not gonna happen." With a gentle laugh, he pulled something from his pocket—the grocery list with Rocky's sketch on the back that she distinctly recalled tossing in the trash can that morning—and laid it on the table in front of her. "I'm no art connoisseur, but I know what I like." He jabbed pencil-Rocky's nose with his index finger. "This is good, *really* good, and don't try to deny it."

She couldn't, not if she was being honest with herself. Even so, she couldn't imagine why anyone would willingly pay twenty dollars for a simple pencil sketch.

Biting her lip, she stood. "You should probably look at some of my other drawings before you pass judgment on whatever talent I may or may not have."

His self-satisfied expression said he'd won—the opening skirmish, anyway. Convincing her to sign up for the church fair would be an uphill battle.

On their way to the study, she realized he'd stopped in the living room, his attention captured by Nana's watercolor portrait of Stormy, a gray-muzzled Lab mix and one of Eventide's first residents. "This is beautiful," he breathed, then pointed to the signature. "Sorcha Madigan?"

"Yes, my grandmother. I'm named for her. Madigan… Maddie. It's an old Irish surname meaning 'little dog.'" She gave a muted laugh. "Fitting, huh?"

"I like it." His warm smile made her pulse beat a little faster. "Artistic talent obviously runs in the family."

She looked away before he could notice the flames rushing up her cheeks.

Flicking on the light in the study, she strode over to the desk. Then, as she was about to hand Witt the sketchbook, she remembered it contained the unfinished drawing of him. She hugged the book to her chest. "Maybe you should let me pick out the best ones to show you."

"Okay." He stretched the word out in a dubious tone as he moved a straight-back side chair closer. Ranger sprawled on the floor beside him.

Taking her seat, she swiveled his direction just enough that he couldn't see as she paged through the sketchbook. Each time she found a drawing she was particularly happy with, she turned it around to show him. After presenting eight or ten sketches, she closed the book and tucked it away in a drawer. "So now you've seen my doodles."

Hands braced on his thighs, he leaned toward her, his expression hardening. "If I ever again hear you referring to those works of art as doodles, so help me—" He clamped his lips together, then took a deep breath before continuing in a kinder tone. "You may not be the fundraiser your grandmother was, but there's money in your drawings. Maddie, please, you have to sign up for the fair. Consider it an experiment, a trial run just to see how it goes. It's one weekend, not a lifetime commitment."

No, her *lifetime commitment* was to the dogs and her grandmother's legacy. But if he was right about the money, how could she afford to pass up such an opportunity? She tapped nervous fingers on the desk. "I have to think."

Witt nodded his understanding. "Don't think too long, though. The fair's less than a month away." He stood and signaled Ranger with a pat of his leg. "We'll head up to the loft now. See you in the morning."

"Good night," she replied absently.

Her gaze drifted toward the drawer where she'd stashed her sketchbook. When was the last time anyone really believed in her this way? Not since Nana, that was for certain. Even Julia, her very best friend in the world, tended to be more of a protector than an encourager.

But Witt…oh, Witt. This man she barely knew was already changing her life in ways she'd never have imagined.

Chapter Five

Two days later, Witt handed Maddie's completed vendor application to Mrs. Caldwell. He still couldn't believe Maddie'd actually filled it out, much less given him the okay to submit it.

"This is wonderful," the woman said as she perused the form. "I've been saving the ideal booth space just for her."

"And you'll waive the fee?" Witt said, hopeful she hadn't had second thoughts about her offer.

"Knowing our typical clientele, I have no doubt the church's percentage will more than compensate." Mrs. Caldwell tucked the application into a folder, then handed him another printed page. "These are our vendor instructions. They're pretty straightforward, but since Ms. McNeill hasn't done anything like this before, I'd be happy to go over everything with her in person."

"I'll let her know."

All Witt had left to do on the deck was apply the waterproof stain. The work went smoothly, and he was on his way home by early afternoon, a good thing since his mood had dipped when he'd remembered what day it was…and what had happened on this date seven years ago.

While he cleaned up in the loft, his Happy's Helpers app notified him of a five-star review from the Caldwells. It wasn't his first high rating, and usually they lifted his spirits, but on this day, David Caldwell's praise struck a bittersweet chord:

> Witt's honest evaluation of our repair project and his concern for doing the job right while keeping costs down showed true integrity. His courtesy, craftsmanship and principled professionalism are exemplary, and we could not be more pleased with his work.

Sinking onto the bed, he closed his eyes. *Integrity... principled.* Those were mighty big words to live up to. He wanted to be worthy of them, and he'd certainly tried over the past couple of years. But believing he could be that kind of man again—if he ever had been—was hard, so very hard.

He could feel the old, familiar darkness creeping in, the craving for a drink so powerful that if there'd been a liquor bottle within reach, he wasn't sure he could withstand temptation. *Why now, Lord, when I've worked so hard to beat this? Help me...help me.*

The things he'd done, the things he'd left undone, the loved ones he'd hurt...he just wanted to forget. Folding in on himself, he slumped onto his side, hardly aware when Ranger whimpered and crawled onto the bed next to him.

Sometime later, he awoke to someone shaking him and a woman's voice calling his name with increasing urgency. Confused, disoriented, he rolled onto his back. The room lay in shadows, and he couldn't make out a face. "Linda?"

"No, it's Maddie." The bedside lamp came on, lighting her red-gold hair. "Witt, what's wrong? Are you sick?"

Awareness slowly returned, but before he could form a reply, a furry paw landed on his chest. The dog's panting breath blew hot and moist across his cheek. He hooked his arm around Ranger's neck. "I'm okay, boy. I'm okay."

"Are you sure?" Maddie's chin quivered. "I waited supper on you, but you never came down. Then Ranger came barking at my back door. I was afraid you were—" She shuddered.

He forced himself to sit up, but embarrassment made it hard to look at her. "Sorry. I—I fell asleep. What time is it?"

"It's almost eight o'clock." Fists on her hips, she stared at him. "I realize I've only known you a couple of weeks, but this just doesn't seem like you. You really scared me."

No more than he'd scared himself. At least the worst had passed, thanks be to God and for the realization that someone in this world actually cared.

Ranger nuzzled his hand, those big brown eyes seeming to convey a directive: *Tell her the truth.*

He owed her that much and more. Exhaling softly, he lifted his gaze to hers. "I had a moment this afternoon. I got sucked down into an emotional black hole, a dark and ugly place I've been too many times to count." Throat closing, he had to look away again. "Just when I think I've broken its power over me, it sneaks up and swallows me whole."

"Oh, Witt…" The compassion in her tone nearly

undid him. She sat by him on the bed, Ranger between them, and rested her arm across his shoulders.

How long they stayed that way, he couldn't say. There was comfort in the silence, strength in her nearness. He didn't know what name to give his growing feelings for her—he only knew that day by day, she was filling up the empty places in his heart.

His stomach growled, breaking the pleasant silence.

Maddie chuckled and reached for his hand. "I kept your supper in the oven. Come down and eat something."

He'd quickly grown to love the cozy, welcoming warmth of her kitchen. He loved watching her stir up tempting aromas on the stove while insisting what a lousy cook she was. He loved sitting across the table from her and laughing over something one of the dogs had done or planning the next day's task list.

Yes, despite today's setback, something about Maddie McNeill was helping him heal.

She set a plate of meat loaf, mashed potatoes and green beans in front of him. "It's a little dried out from sitting in the oven for over two hours."

"You won't hear any complaints from me." Scooting up to the table, he lowered his head to offer silent thanks—for the food, for Maddie, for the God who never left him in his brokenness.

Maddie went to the pantry and returned with a small handful of homemade dog biscuits. When she took her chair, Ranger plopped down in front of her, tail wagging and an expectant look on his face. "Yes, these are for you, fella." She offered him one and then another. "A smart, loyal dog like you deserves a reward."

"You're spoiling him," Witt said over a mouthful of meat loaf.

"And you don't?" She scoffed. "I don't imagine he's slept in his own bed a single night since you two moved into the loft."

She had him there.

After he'd eaten a few more bites, she quietly asked, "Who's Linda?"

Taking a shallow breath, he stabbed a green bean. "Where'd you hear that name?"

"From you." Eyes lowered, Maddie drew invisible circles on the table with the tip of her finger. "When I tried to wake you, you called me Linda. So I figured she must mean something to you."

He laid aside his fork. "Linda was my wife. I haven't seen her or my kids since she threw me out."

"I'm so sorry, Witt. How long has it been?"

"Almost eight years." He closed his eyes briefly. "It was seven years ago today that our divorce became final."

Maddie's quiet nod was all the sympathy he could handle. Finishing his meal, he nudged the plate away. "Thank you. That hit the spot."

"If you'd like something sweet, I have fig cookie bars in the pantry." She hopped up from the table. "I'll start some decaf to go with them."

"Don't trouble yourself, Maddie. I've inconvenienced you enough already."

Before he could rise, she halted him with a hand on his shoulder. "Please stay. I don't think you should be alone tonight."

He looked at her askance but saw only kindness in her shimmering turquoise eyes.

She gasped as if realizing how her invitation may have sounded. "I—I only meant we could talk a little longer. Or watch TV. Or play cribbage or something." Her chest caved. "I'm concerned for you, Witt. I know firsthand how hard certain anniversaries can be, and this has clearly been a difficult one for you."

Maybe it'd be best if he did stick around a bit longer. Decaf and cribbage with Maddie would be a lot safer than returning to the loft with only his dog and his regrets for company. With a grateful smile, he stood. "You start the coffee. I'll get the cookies."

An hour later, after she'd gleefully trounced him in three straight games, he slapped his cards on the table and cast her a mock scowl. "I thought the idea was for you to cheer me up."

"What—I should let you win just so you feel better?" Grinning, she plucked the pegs from the game board and tucked them into the storage slot on the back.

"Wouldn't hurt," he muttered with a wink. He wound a rubber band around the stack of playing cards.

She harrumphed. "There's a little coffee left in the pot. Want to help me finish it?"

"Sure. Thanks." When she'd refilled their mugs and returned to her chair, he reached across the table to touch her arm. "Really, Maddie, thank you. Spending this evening with you has meant more than I can say."

"You're welcome." Smiling, she sipped her decaf. After a moment, she began hesitantly, "If it's too hard, I understand, but…would you tell me about your family, your children?"

Fingers wrapped around his mug, he drew a breath. "Emily was barely sixteen when I left. I remember she'd just gotten her driver's license. Trent was twelve and practically a virtuoso on the piano."

Maddie skewed her lips. "So that'd make them twenty-three and nineteen now. After all these years, are you sure they wouldn't want to reconnect?"

The confused and angry expressions on his kids' faces the last time he'd seen them were burned into his memory. Right in front of them, and drunk as a skunk, he'd had his final big blowup with Linda. He'd called his wife names no spouse should ever use, no child should ever hear. Linda had lashed back with a well-deserved slap to his face and a few ugly names of her own. Then she'd given him an ultimatum: leave under his own power or she'd call the police and have him hauled away. Either way, she warned him never to come near her or their children again.

Meeting Maddie's gaze, he cast her a sad smile. "Yep, I'm a hundred percent certain that my children would want nothing to do with me."

She didn't believe him, not for an instant. No matter how bad things got, or how much time had passed, children never stopped wishing they could set things right with their parents. It didn't matter that Maddie's father had walked out before she'd had a chance to know him. It didn't matter that her mother never figured out the whole single-parent thing and had dumped her on Nana. Mom was living in Tucson now with her boyfriend du jour, and Daddy had vanished into the ether, leaving Maddie with nothing but his last name and a few faded snapshots. Yet even now, what she wouldn't give for the chance to show them what she'd made of her life in spite of how they'd failed her.

Forgiveness, however? That was another issue altogether.

But why did it have to be that way for Witt? Maybe he'd made mistakes—bad ones, she gathered—but she didn't have to know him back then to appreciate the effort he put forth every day to rise above those mistakes and become a better person.

When the old chime clock in the living room struck half past ten, Witt said he'd imposed long enough. He thanked her again for her kindness and excused himself to return to the loft. She only hoped she hadn't made things worse again by bringing up his family. He did seem slightly more at peace, though...or was he only resigned?

She didn't see much of him over the next few days. On Friday, he got an emergency repair call that turned into a two-day job, so he hit the road again early Saturday morning after apologizing profusely for leaving her with all the kennel chores. He returned to Missoula on Sunday to attend church with friends from the transitional home and then stayed for the celebration honoring one of them for earning his GED.

Pacing the quiet house that afternoon, Maddie had to admit she'd quickly grown accustomed to having someone else around. Anytime Witt had business elsewhere, she'd begun to feel his absence acutely.

She picked up the phone and called Julia. "What's up with you?"

"I'm in my backyard pulling weeds. Wanna come help?"

"I hope you're not pulling dandelions. You're supposed to leave them for the bees."

"I'll leave a patch by the back fence, okay?" Her

words were breathy with exertion. "I just prefer not having to wade through a jungle every time I let the twins out for a run."

Julia's cuddly, short-legged dachshunds had become the center of her world—away from the veterinary practice, anyway—ever since her son had been killed in a motorcycle accident last year. "Maybe I will come over. I haven't seen Daisy and Dash in a while, and the walls are starting to close in."

Twenty minutes later, she parked in Julia's driveway and made her way to the backyard, where she was greeted by the two yapping brownish-red pups. "Hey, kiddos!" She knelt to give them some pats. "Keeping your mom out of trouble?"

"Or making more trouble than they're worth." Julia rose from her crouch with a handful of weeds, the roots dripping clumps of soil. "I'm done for the day. Let me clean up and we can visit."

Shortly they were seated in Julia's sunny den with glasses of iced tea and each with a dog on her lap. Stroking Daisy's floppy ears, Maddie pursed her lips. "Well, I've gone and done it now."

"Uh-oh. Something even more out of character than offering your barn loft to a stranger? Please tell me the background check didn't peg him as an escaped convict."

Background check? The thought had never occurred to her, although it probably should have. She'd surprised herself at how easily she'd given Witt the benefit of the doubt. "No, no, nothing like that. Actually, I've signed up for a booth at the Trinity Fellowship Memorial Day Arts and Crafts Fair. I'm hoping it'll bring in a little money for the sanctuary."

"Seriously?" Julia's sputter startled Dash, who yelped and leaped to the floor. "I thought fundraising gave you nightmares."

"Still does. But this is a little different." She grimaced, because what she'd agreed to do was almost as scary. "I'll be doing on-the-spot pet portraits."

"Oh, Maddie, how fun! It's about time you quit hiding your talent in a desk drawer. Who convinced you to—" Julia palmed her forehead. "Wait, don't tell me. *Witt?*"

"Yes, Witt. And don't give me that look." She told how he'd learned about the opportunity from one of his handyman clients.

Lifting Dash back onto her lap, Julia frowned. "I still have misgivings about the guy, but I have to give him credit."

"If you'd only get to know him, you'd see for yourself what a good man he is."

"For your sake, I hope he's every bit as decent and respectable as you claim. But you and I have both been burned by trusting the wrong men. And when I think of how that crooked investment manager cheated your grandparents—" Jaw clenched, she looked away. "I'd hate for you to be taken in by another swindling lowlife."

"You don't have to worry. Believe me, I've got my eyes wide open."

"Are you sure? Maddie, you've let Witt into your *home*—a man you've known barely two weeks. You're alone out there. Anything could happen. He could rob you blind. He could murder you in your sleep—"

"Julia. Stop." Palm extended, Maddie shook her head. "I was hoping for a pleasant Sunday afternoon with my best friend. If all you're going to do is harp on my apparent lack of good judgment, I'll leave right now."

"No, please." Julia heaved a contrite sigh. "I got a little carried away. Maybe we should change the subject."

"Good idea. Tell me how things are going at the clinic."

The tension between them eased slightly as Julia began with stories about a couple of her more interesting patients last week. Maddie kept the conversation going by asking about Julia's parents, her partners in the Frasier Family Veterinary Clinic. They were nearing retirement age, and naturally Julia had concerns about eventually taking on full responsibility for the practice.

"It was always going to be Steven and me." Eyes welling, she ran her fingers along Dash's spine. "A couple of years from now, he would have completed his veterinary degree at Washington State."

"I know you miss him," Maddie murmured. She wished she could ease her friend's sorrow. Giving Daisy a chin scratch, she had an idea. She carried the dog over to Julia's chair and situated her in Julia's lap next to Dash.

Her friend looked up in confusion. "You're not leaving already?"

"No, of course not." Stepping back, she studied the arrangement, then shifted Dash slightly. "You're going to be my practice models. Can I borrow a pencil and paper?"

Julia pointed her to a drawer in a side table. "Wait, shouldn't I fix my hair or something?"

"I'm not taking your photograph. When I'm finished, you'll look perfectly coiffed, I promise."

Sitting across from them, Maddie began her sketch.

Before she'd attempted Witt's portrait, her subjects had mainly been dogs. Maybe it was time to stretch herself a little.

Humph, like she hadn't been doing a lot of that already in the past couple of weeks!

At the sight of Witt's truck next to the barn, Maddie's heart lifted. Leaving Julia's, and with no idea when to expect him back, she'd been dreading the return to a lonely house. After parking the aging Suburban in the carport, she strode to the kennel, where she found Witt measuring out the dogs' evening meals.

She joined him at the counter and began organizing meds and supplements. "Have a nice visit with your friends?"

"Yeah. It was good to catch up with everyone— and to finally introduce them to Ranger, after they'd heard me talk about him so much." He scooped some of Boots's pureed food into the toothless sheltie's bowl. "How was your day? Did you go to church?"

"No, I, um, took care of a few things around here." He'd asked her last Sunday about which church she belonged to and if he could go along. She'd made a lame excuse that time, too, but after Nana's death, returning to church had been too fraught with memories. Shifting the conversation, she said, "I went over to Julia's this afternoon. She has a pair of cute dachshunds, so I sketched her with them."

Starting out to the dog runs with a tray of food bowls, he smiled over his shoulder. "I'd like to see it sometime."

Witt didn't have much else to say as they completed the kennel tasks. His return to the transitional home seemed to have brought on a pensive mood. After his despondency a few days ago, and knowing he was an admitted alcoholic, should she be worried?

On their way to the pasture to bring in the horses, she asked if he had any special requests for supper, then grinned and added with a snort, "Not that I can promise to fulfill them."

"Sure don't need much. I had a big meal with the guys earlier. Carl loves to grill, so we had burgers, brats, chicken—the works."

"Hmmm, no veggies? Sounds like a salad night."

Witt laughed, a pleasant sound after his relative silence. "Sounds about right."

After supper, she tried to talk him into another game of cribbage, but he claimed fatigue and planned to turn in early. When he got up to leave, she followed him through the mudroom. Stopping him at the back door, she asked, "Witt, are you okay?"

One hand resting on Ranger's head, he looked toward the setting sun and hauled in a deep breath. "Yeah, I'm okay." He turned his smile upon Maddie. "Being back with the guys today reminded me how far I've come in two years. I've still got a long way to go—my lapse the other night proved it—but every day is progress. What more can I ask?"

"I suppose that's one way to look at it." She shrugged and glanced away. "But there are days when progress is mighty hard to see."

Head cocked, he studied her. "Guess I should be asking if *you're* okay."

"Me?" Her gaze drifted toward the kennel. "As long as the future of those dogs is at stake, I'll never really be okay."

Chapter Six

Days later, Witt still recalled the despair in Maddie's eyes that Sunday evening. More unsettling, he couldn't shake the memory of how badly he'd wanted to take her in his arms. Hold her...reassure her...kiss her.

Thoughts he had no right to entertain, much less ever dream of acting on. Even on the slightest chance she could someday be interested in him as a man, he had nothing to offer. He was a middle-aged nobody with a messy past, a minuscule bank account and zero prospects beyond his handyman job.

Installing a client's new garbage disposal, he looked over at Ranger, whom the homeowner had kindly consented to allow inside since the early-May weather had turned nasty. "I hope you're not getting too attached to country living, boy, because we should probably start looking for our own place in town soon."

It was either that or keep tripping over these growing feelings for Maddie.

He crawled out from under the sink and tried the disposal. It hummed like a luxury sedan. "All set, Mrs.

Bartlett. This one should keep you in business for another ten years."

"Thank you, Witt." The petite white-haired woman handed him her credit card.

As he calculated the bill and ran the card, he could feel her staring at him. "Something wrong, ma'am?"

"You remind me of someone, and I can't place who it is. Have you always lived around Missoula?"

"Uh, no." Such questions always made him uneasy. Though he'd made his way to Missoula after losing his job and family in Butte, he dreaded one day being recognized by a former client. *Bartlett*... The name didn't ring a bell. But that didn't mean much, considering all the years he'd spent in an alcoholic stupor. "Here's your card, ma'am. The receipt should already be in your email inbox."

"Happy's Helpers always treats us right. A shame all companies aren't as honest and reliable. My husband and I got burned pretty badly by a Butte investment company several years back."

"Yes, ma'am." He swallowed painfully and finished packing his tools and supplies. "I'll be on my way, then. Thanks for your business, Mrs. Bartlett."

She walked him to the door. "We've mostly recovered—knew better than to put all our eggs in one basket—but I've been leery of scammers ever since."

"Understandable." His stomach was starting to cramp. He zipped up his jacket and tugged his baseball cap from the pocket. "Let's go, Ranger."

"You might have heard about it in the news." Apparently, she had plenty more to say on the subject. "It was awful what they did to unsuspecting folks like us, hardworking people just hoping to build toward a comfortable retirement. I'm glad they threw the book at those skunks. Every last one of 'em deserves to be locked away for life."

Witt knew firsthand that most of them had been locked away—the ones directly involved, anyway. And though life sentences hadn't been on the books, they wouldn't be free to swindle anyone else for a good long time.

On the other hand, Witt would be serving time for the rest of his days. After he'd discovered what was going on at Copper Bluff Financial Professionals, he'd reported it to the federal and state authorities. They advised him to remain anonymous to protect his family from retribution, but even so, when the mud started flying, he got splattered. Once other investment firms learned of his connection with the company, he became persona non grata. Out of work, his reputation destroyed, he'd begun the downhill slide that cost him everything he had left.

He tuned out whatever else Mrs. Bartlett was saying. Slapping on his ball cap with one hand, he hefted his toolbox with the other. "Sorry to rush off. Got another call to make this afternoon."

He'd let one of the other handymen take any future calls from the Bartletts.

His next job was back at the Caldwells' to install a new ceiling fan in their great room. After only a few minutes in their affirming presence, he'd put Mrs. Bartlett's unwelcome reminders out of his mind.

"I hope your friend Maddie is getting excited about the fair," Mrs. Caldwell said as he worked. "We've included her booth in recent publicity, and the response has been enthusiastic."

"I'll be sure and tell her." Witt fastened another blade onto the new fan. He only hoped Maddie wasn't on the verge of backing out, because the closer it came to Memorial Day, the more anxious she seemed. "I'd still like to get Maddie over here to meet you and maybe get some advice about what to expect."

"We should meet at the church so I can show her around. How about tomorrow morning, say...ten o'clock?"

"I'll text her right now."

Maddie didn't reply right away—he'd forgotten this time of the afternoon she was usually online doing her tutoring. He was just finishing up with the ceiling fan when his phone buzzed.

It was a nonanswer. Let's talk about it over supper.

Mrs. Caldwell must have noticed his frown. "Everything all right?"

"It's Maddie. I'm afraid she's getting cold feet."

The woman gave a thoughtful nod. "You get her to the church in the morning. I'll handle the rest."

Alicia Caldwell sounded like exactly the kind of person Maddie needed in her life—someone with a slightly more positive attitude than her overprotective friend Julia. Witt liked the veterinarian well enough, what little he'd seen of her, but he got the feeling she had issues of her own. Her overly cautious outlook could easily sway Maddie in the wrong direction.

"No, I'm not chickening out," Maddie insisted. At least she hadn't yet, although the thought had crossed her mind. More than once.

Witt served himself a spoonful of mixed veggies. "I certainly hope not." Softening his tone, he went on, "Once you've seen the facility and met with Mrs. Caldwell, you'll feel a lot more at ease."

"If you say so." She grimaced. "All right, I'll go, but I'm only doing it for the dogs." *Doing it for the dogs* had become her mantra over the past several days. It was the only way she could even think about putting her drawings on display and expecting people to pay money for what, to her, was only a pastime.

Ten o'clock Friday morning found them at Trinity Fellowship Church on the outskirts of Missoula. Maddie had decided against her usual attire of faded jeans and an oversize flannel shirt, and instead wore nicer jeans and a navy-and-white-striped pullover. Her hair was what it was, an unruly reddish-blond mop held in check with a scrunchie.

When Alicia Caldwell met them at the entrance to the gym, she wished she'd taken much more time with her appearance. Dressed in a violet tunic top over sleek black ankle pants, the slender, dark-haired woman looked like she could be a sixtysomething model for a fashion magazine.

"Hello, Witt. And you must be Maddie." She offered a welcoming smile. "I've been looking forward to meeting you."

All too conscious of the extra couple of pounds she'd put on over the winter, Maddie tugged on the hem of her shirt. "I suppose Witt's told you I'm a little uncomfortable with this whole thing."

To her credit, the woman didn't immediately reply with empty reassurance. She gave the ever-present Ranger a friendly pat, then pulled open one of the glass doors. "Come inside. I'll show you around and tell you a little more about our event, and you can jump in with any questions you have."

So far out of her depth, Maddie wasn't sure she could come up with an intelligent question to ask. For most of the tour, she simply smiled and nodded while taking copious mental notes.

Witt seemed to have somewhat of a clue, at least. "Good idea putting Maddie's booth at the end of the main aisle."

"Yes, it should give her plenty of visibility but in a position where her customers won't impede the flow."

He scratched his chin. "She'll need some kind of sign."

"Definitely. Hang anything you want on the back wall. And you should display some of your previous work, too, Maddie."

She squinted one eye. "Um, which *work*, exactly? Because all I really have is what's in my sketchbooks. And come to think of it, Mrs. Caldwell—"

"Please, call me Alicia."

"Alicia. If I'm not mistaken, the only one of my sketches you've ever seen is the tiny one Witt showed you on the back of a grocery list. How can you be sure I won't be a complete flop?"

Alicia tilted her head and smiled. "Because I know artistic talent when I see it, even in a tiny sketch. And if Witt says there's more where that came from, I have no reason to doubt him."

A satisfied grin spread across Witt's face. More like *self*-satisfied, in Maddie's opinion. She chewed her lip as another thought occurred. "Okay, but if I'm drawing pictures, I'll need someone else to handle money."

Witt opened his mouth to speak, then hesitated. "You should get your friend Julia to help."

"I'll ask her, but on holidays she's usually on call for veterinary emergencies, so she might have to leave at a moment's notice. But you'll be there, won't you?" She knelt to give Ranger a scratch behind the ears. "I was counting on you bringing this guy along to be my 'spokesdog.'"

Alicia laughed. "Perfect! If business slows, you can sketch Ranger as a way to entice people to stop by."

"But since you'll be gone all day," Witt began, "somebody ought to stay at the sanctuary. I was thinking I'd look after things there."

He was right—she couldn't leave the dogs unattended for hours on end, a problem that hadn't occurred to her until now. "Maybe you could come for part of the day, though, especially if Julia gets called away?"

"Yeah." His glance shifted sideways. "We'll figure something out."

Why did he sound as if he'd rather *not* work in the booth with her? He'd gotten her into this, after all.

She returned her attention to Alicia, who had a few more tips to share. But at home later, as she and Witt attended to evening kennel chores, she confronted him.

"Is there more to it?" she asked.

Scooping kibble into a bowl, he shot her a confused frown. "More to what?"

"Are the dogs the only reason you didn't want to help me at the fair?"

He laid aside the scoop and pressed his palms atop the counter. "I'd very much like to be with you at the fair. But besides the fact that the dogs need tending, I…" He blew out sharply and lowered his head. "I had a bit of a scare yesterday. At one of my service calls, I was afraid the lady recognized me from...before."

"Before. You mean from your past life?" Maddie touched his arm. "What happened? Did she say anything?"

"Only that I reminded her of someone. And I can't honestly say I didn't remember her. So much of that time has become a blur." He shifted to face her. "I always knew this could happen, but by the time I started working for Happy's Helpers, I figured living on the street had aged me enough that the chances of being recognized were pretty slim."

She could see how bothered he was. "But it's been so long. Would it really matter after all this time?"

Several seconds passed before he replied, and the struggle behind his expression tore at Maddie's heart. "Losing my job eight years ago destroyed me. Worse, I let it destroy my family. Even after rehab and my two years at the transitional home and all the counseling and support I got there, every reminder of the past is like a punch to the gut."

"I'm so sorry, Witt." Her hand found his on the edge of the counter. His fingers were cool, and she tried to warm them with her own. "This is why you'd rather not be with me at the fair, because you're worried someone might recognize you?"

"It's a long shot, I know, but...yes."

She wanted to ask him more, insist he tell her what awful thing had happened that had cost him his career and family. He'd assured her he didn't have a criminal background...but what, then? Because it had to have been something unspeakably bad to still haunt him after all these years. Someday, she hoped he'd trust her enough to tell her about it.

Witt was getting real tired of letting his personal issues bring Maddie down. Instead of worrying over him, she should be looking forward to the fair and using her artistic talent to raise money for the sanctuary. Over the next few days, he made an effort to be as upbeat as possible, encouraging her every chance he got.

During their meeting with Alicia Caldwell, the woman had mentioned a printing company that offered discounts to vendors for signs, banners and other fair-related needs. On Monday, in town for a service call, Witt stopped by the place. He'd just gotten his weekly Happy's Helpers check, so he wanted to surprise Maddie with a sign for her booth.

A medium-size vinyl banner with grommets for hanging seemed affordable. The printing company rep showed him a selection of generic logos, and he selected one depicting three different-size dogs. For wording, he decided on:

EVENTIDE DOG SANCTUARY
Your purchase from artist and owner Maddie McNeill helps support these special animals!

The rep promised delivery by the end of the week. In the meantime, Witt had another idea he wanted to work on, but it would require Maddie's cooperation.

"I need a few of your drawings," he said as they cleaned up the kitchen after supper that evening.

One eye narrowed, she set a plate in the cupboard. "For what?"

"Remember, we talked about this on Friday with Alicia. You should have some of your drawings on display so customers can see examples of your work."

"I told you, all I have is what's in my sketchbooks."

"So tear out a few and let me frame them. I'll use some of that scrap wood from the barn. The weathered wood will set off your pencil drawings perfectly."

"Angus Wittenbauer, you are something else," she said with a laugh. "Okay, okay, let me finish here and we'll go pick some out."

He usually cringed at being called by his real name, but from Maddie, for some reason, he found it endearing…irresistible. Warmth engulfed him, a heady sensation of pure happiness.

Dropping flatware into a drawer, she studied him. "What are you grinning about?"

"I, ah…" He pulled a hand down his face, as if he could wipe away the feelings he couldn't seem to keep a lid on. If only he could forget everything from before the moment he'd walked into her life. If only his whole world could begin and end right here with Maddie McNeill.

She turned away abruptly and cleared her throat. "I'll go get my sketchbooks."

Did she sense it, too, this…whatever it was…growing between them? He'd been telling himself he should find another place to live, but he just couldn't make himself do it.

Ranger whined and bumped his leg. He returned to his chair and pressed the dog's furry face between his palms. "I know, fella. Believe me, I know. The longer we stay here, the harder it's gonna be to leave."

"Leave?"

He hadn't heard Maddie returning, and her anxious look shot an arrow through his heart. "Yeah, to go up to the loft," he said with a nervous laugh. "Once I start looking at your pictures, I won't want to quit."

With a doubtful frown, she marched to the table and laid the sketchbooks in front of him. While he began paging through them, she sat down and crossed her arms. "How many are you thinking to use?"

"Maybe six or eight?" In only moments, he'd become engrossed in the images. "This is Boots, right? And I love this full-size sketch of Rocky. Can I use these?"

"I guess so."

He carefully tore along the perforation and laid the drawings aside, then continued browsing. "There's a page missing here. Did you already remove one?"

"Oh. That." She gave a dismissive shrug. "It was something different I was trying. Not one of the dogs."

"Branching out, eh? Maybe you'll show me sometime."

Her quick smile and arched brow clearly communicated, *Don't count on it.*

He selected a few more drawings that caught his eye, three of which were of dogs from before his time. Sadness filled Maddie's expression as she glanced at them and nodded her consent. Her affection for the animals never failed to tug at his emotions.

Straightening the stack of eight sketches, he said, "These'll do fine. I'll get started framing them right after kennel chores tomorrow."

"What, no handyman calls?"

"I've stayed pretty busy the past couple of weeks. Wouldn't hurt to take a day off every once in a while.

Besides, the fair's only two weeks away, and I want to give you as much help getting ready as I can."

"You're already doing more than I have any right to expect." She touched his hand, the shimmer in her eyes making him suck in a breath. "Honestly, Witt, if it had been anyone else answering my roof repair call, I don't know what I'd be doing right now. Certainly not contemplating selling my drawings at an arts and crafts fair."

"If not that, then something else. You'd never let the dogs down, whatever it takes." Needing to lighten the mood, he released a chuckle. "I do know you'd probably still have a warped floor, a couple of wonky doorknobs…" Using his fingers, he ticked off several more repairs he'd done around the place.

A hearty laugh burst from her throat. "Stop! You've made your point and confirmed mine. I'd be utterly lost without you."

Until those last words, he'd been laughing with her. They both went suddenly silent, lips parted, breath quickening. He bolted upright, his chair screeching across the tile. "It's late. I should get upstairs." Backing toward the door, he patted his thigh. "Ranger, let's go."

Outside in the chilly night air, he could finally grab a full breath. He might be all wrong for Maddie, but not even a herd of stampeding buffalo could drag him away. Unless and until she outright told him to go, he knew now that he could never make himself leave.

Utterly lost without you.

Had she really said those words aloud? Minutes after watching Witt hurry out, Maddie's heart was still hammering. She'd never meant to imply anything romantic in that statement. But it was true nonetheless. True in ways she couldn't fully fathom.

Maybe a cup of chamomile tea would slow her pulse and calm her racing thoughts. She lit a flame under the teakettle, then went to gather her sketchbooks. The drawings Witt had chosen still lay on the table, and with a quiet sigh, she paged through them. These were definitely among her favorites and some of her best work.

The kettle whistled. She poured boiling water over a tea bag, then carried the mug and her sketchbooks to the study. Before storing the tablets in the drawer, she withdrew the portrait of Witt she'd torn out and hidden away at the very bottom. One look at those haunting eyes looking back at her, and her emotions surged all over again.

He was a special man, selfless and thoughtful and good. The kind of man she'd long ago decided didn't exist in her world, not since her grandfather, anyway. But as Julia continually reminded her, what did she *really* know about Angus Wittenbauer? He'd been forthcoming about his job loss, his divorce and estrangement from his children, his alcoholism and homelessness. Even so, there remained big chunks of his life he wouldn't talk about.

And honesty meant everything to Maddie.

Six years later, she could still recall the look on Garrett's face. She'd taught her last English class on a Friday morning and had decided to drive over to the UCLA campus to surprise him and maybe go out to dinner. She'd never been to his home or office before—he'd always been so considerate about coming to Whittier for their dates so she wouldn't have to fight the freeway traffic.

He'd stepped out for a moment, so she'd used the time to take in the surroundings of the intelligent, sophisticated scholar she'd fallen in love with—the man she'd felt certain was on the verge of proposing.

Then she saw it, a framed studio portrait of Garrett wearing the expensive blue tapestry-print tie she'd given him for Christmas—and gazing into the eyes of the attractive and equally sophisticated blonde at his side! Three smiling, well-dressed children clustered around them.

He'd returned just then. Eyes widening like a cornered animal, he'd frozen. "*Maddie. What are you doing here?*"

She hadn't been able to think of a coherent response. Smashing the portrait against his chest, she'd stormed out.

It had taken her less than a day to verify her discovery, but months to process the betrayal. Now, all these years later, she still struggled with trust.

Again, her gaze fell to the drawing of Witt. No matter how hard she looked, she couldn't detect the smallest flicker of deceit. Would he finally be the one to break through her barriers and make her believe in true love again?

Laughing to herself, she shook her head. "Mr. Wittenbauer, you're already off to a very good start."

Chapter Seven

It was the Saturday of Memorial Day weekend. As Maddie darted around preparing for the fair on Monday, she could barely contain the butterflies swarming in her stomach. Witt had done a beautiful job framing her sketches, even made little easels so she could display them on the table in her booth.

Moments ago, he'd presented her with the banner he'd ordered. All she could think about was how Nana would have loved it. One of the dogs in the logo even resembled Joey.

"It's perfect, Witt. Thank you." After another appreciative look, she started to roll up the banner. "I'll pay you back out of my earnings."

He stayed her hand. "Didn't you hear me? I said it's a gift."

"But you've been working so hard to build your savings. Plus all the things you've done around here would have cost me ten times as much if you hadn't taken care of them."

"You've done so much more for me." His fingers tightened around hers, sending a pleasant shiver up her spine. Just as quickly, he let go and stepped back. "So. What else can I do to help you get ready?"

Missing his touch, she returned to rolling up the banner. "I need to recheck my box of drawing supplies, but it's about time to let the dogs have some playtime. Would you mind watching them in the yard for a bit? Just the big kids. We'll take the littles out later."

"On it." He gave a mock salute and bustled off to the kennel.

In the study, she recounted her pencils and added them to the box with the new Strathmore 400 sketch pads she'd splurged on last week. With twenty-four pages in each, she should have enough for ninety-six pet portraits—provided she didn't ruin any and have to start over. If she sold even a third that many drawings, it would be a day well spent.

She pressed a hand to her stomach as a fresh wave of doubt surged. She was an English teacher, not an artist. Who was she kidding?

How late was too late to back out?

"Maddie?" Witt's voice came from the kitchen.

"In the study," she called.

Seconds later, he stood in the doorway. "You'd better come to the kennel. It's Joey."

Her heart plummeted. "What's happened?"

"He collapsed in the play yard. I carried him back to his run, but he's breathing really hard and acting weak and confused."

She ran past him, grabbing her cell phone on the way and hitting the speed dial for Julia. Her friend answered as she reached the kennel. "Can you come over? Something's wrong with Joey."

"I'm at the clinic, but we're just about to close for the day. Tell me what's going on."

Entering Joey's run, Maddie knelt to comfort the panting dog while she repeated what Witt had said.

"Maddie, I don't want you to panic—" Julia's tone was calm yet insistent "—but it'd be best if you bring Joey straight to the clinic. I'll wait for you here."

"O-okay." *Don't panic?* Her heart was already about to explode. Disconnecting, she looked up at Witt. "Can you help me get him into the Suburban?"

"Tell me where your keys are. I'll bring the car closer."

"They're in the front pocket of my purse. I think I left it in the study."

Within minutes, she heard the old vehicle rumble up near the kennel door. Witt came in and gently lifted Joey from his bed. "I'll drive. Grab his blanket. You can sit with him in the back seat."

She climbed in first and spread out the blanket. Witt eased the whimpering dog onto the seat, his head resting on her lap. When Witt opened the driver's door, Ranger leaped across to the passenger side, then poked his head between the seat backs. Looking from Joey to Maddie and whining softly, he seemed as worried about the old white shepherd as she was.

Witt drove with cautious haste, careful on the turns, faster on the straightaways, as Maddie directed him to the Frasier Veterinary Clinic. This was her first real crisis with the dogs since Nana had died, and she couldn't begin to describe what a comfort it was to have Witt's strength to lean on.

At the clinic, a vet tech held the door as Witt carried Joey inside, then showed them to an exam room. Moments later, Julia entered. She smiled briefly, but her expression turned grim as she checked Joey's vitals, palpated his abdomen and gently looked inside his mouth. Maddie didn't need veterinary training to know his ghostly pale gums weren't a good sign.

"What is it?" she asked, fearful of the answer.

Julia stroked the dog's head. "I won't know for sure until I do imaging and run a few more tests, but his symptoms are consistent with internal bleeding from a ruptured splenic tumor."

Maddie could hardly breathe. "A tumor—*cancer*?"

"Not necessarily, but...more likely than not. Either way, without immediate surgery to remove the spleen, Joey won't survive the next few hours."

She clenched her jaw to keep from crying out. This was one more loss she couldn't deal with. "How...how much would it cost?"

Julia glanced away, then stated a figure, no doubt greatly discounted from what anyone else would be charged. Even so, the number made Maddie gasp.

Witt came up beside her, his hand resting firmly on her shoulder. He didn't have to say anything. His presence was reassurance enough.

She hiked her chin. "Do whatever it takes to save him."

Later, when she was thinking more clearly, she'd figure out how she'd pay for it.

At Julia's nod, Witt ushered Maddie to the waiting room and sat beside her on one of the padded benches. When she collapsed against him, he wrapped his arms around her and tucked her close. "It'll be okay."

It wasn't quite how he'd imagined someday holding her like this. And oh, yes, he'd definitely thought about it. But all she needed in this moment was comfort, and he'd offer what little he could.

His thoughts returned to what he'd seen on her desk when he'd gone looking for her purse. To find his own face looking back at him had riveted him to the floor. As Maddie had sketched him, the set of his mouth suggested inner resolve shadowed by self-doubt. The eyes held both immeasurable pain and persistent hope.

How had she captured his essence so completely?

Maddie's tremulous sigh returned him to the present. He spied a single-serve beverage machine on the counter, along with an assortment of coffee, hot chocolate and herbal tea pods. Without asking, he eased her off his shoulder, then brewed a cup of lemon-ginger tea for her, strong coffee for himself.

Sitting up, she smiled a weary thank-you as she curled her fingers around the disposable cup. "I'm glad you're here." Ranger rested his chin on her knee, and she gave him a pat. "You and Ranger both."

"Neither of us would be anywhere else."

She sipped her tea and stared at the door to the treatment area. "I'm so scared, Witt. Did I do the right thing? I mean, if Joey's suffering—if it does turn out to be cancer—"

"One step at a time, okay? If Julia didn't believe there was a chance of saving him, don't you think she'd have told you?"

"You're right. But the cost!" She shuddered. When she nearly spilled her tea, she set down the cup on a nearby table. "I'd do absolutely anything for Joey, but it'll take me months to pay down this surgery bill. And if he needs additional treatments, what am I going to do?"

"You're already doing something. The fair on Monday, remember?"

She shook her head briskly. "I can't, not now. Worrying about Joey, I'd be a wreck. There's no way I'd be able to draw."

Her hair had fallen across one eye, and he smoothed it back from her face. Tenderly, he said, "Look at me, Maddie."

Slowly, she obeyed.

His fingers were still entwined in her curls. Tearing his mind away from their silky feel, he drew a steadying breath. "The fair's still two days away, so you don't have to decide anything yet. Let's wait and see what Julia says when the surgery's done. In the meantime, we'll keep praying."

"Praying?" The sound from her throat was somewhere between a laugh and a sob. "I'm trying, but it doesn't feel like God is listening."

He squeezed her hand. "He is. I promise you, He is."

She stood abruptly and paced to the closed door and back, arms locked across her chest. "How much longer? Shouldn't she be finished by now?"

Witt checked his watch. Only about twenty minutes had passed. Julia had said if all went well, the surgery should take about an hour. But Maddie was a coiled spring and not likely to contain herself even another ten minutes. He needed to distract her.

He drained his coffee cup, then tossed it into a nearby trash receptacle. "Come sit down, Maddie. Tell me more about Eventide. Where'd the idea come from? How did your grandparents get it started?"

Maddie blinked. "It's hard now to remember there ever *not* being an Eventide." Returning to the bench, she retrieved her cup of tea and took a thoughtful sip. "My grandparents always had at least two or three dogs on the place. When I came to live with them, I was a lonely and shy six-year-old, and the dogs became my best friends. One of them had puppies, and Nana said I could keep one to raise." Her lips curved into a sad smile. "That pup and I basically grew up together."

"What was its name?"

"Tootsie. She was part spaniel, part whatever the neighbor's mutt was." A faraway look filled her eyes as she absently scratched Ranger's chin. "Curly black-and-white fur, floppy ears and two dime-size black spots on her tongue. The roof of her mouth was solid black, which Nana always said was a sign of a really smart dog. That may be an old wives' tale, but in Tootsie's case, it held true."

Witt chuckled. "I'd have to say it's true of Ranger, too." He needed to keep Maddie talking. "You had Tootsie for a long time?"

"From third grade all through high school. When I went away to college, I left her with my grandparents, but I came home to visit as often as I could."

"She must have been getting pretty old by then."

"She was, but she still greeted me like a frisky puppy every time I walked in the door. I remember one Christmas holiday when I arrived home to Tootsie's excited yipping. Nana said how she wished every elderly pet knew it was loved as much as I loved Tootsie. By the time I came home for spring break, they'd rescued three senior dogs from the shelter, and Grandpa had started building the kennel. The sanctuary just grew from there."

She set her empty cup aside, then tucked her ankle

beneath the opposite thigh so she could peer out the window behind them. "Eventide came to mean everything to my grandparents. Over the years, Nana became an expert at applying for grants and soliciting donations. After Grandpa retired, he wanted to take some of his pension—"

The inner door opened and Julia stepped into the waiting room. "The surgery's done. Joey's resting comfortably."

Maddie sprang to her feet. "Is he going to be okay?"

"I'm hopeful. There was a large mass on his spleen, but I didn't find any other tumors. We won't know if it's malignant until I get the lab results back in a week or so."

"And then?"

Julia gripped Maddie's wrists in a firm but reassuring hold. "Let's just get him over this hump. One step at a time, okay?"

"Advice I've just been given for the second time today." Maddie glanced back at Witt and offered a quick smile. To Julia, she said, "So what is the next step?"

"I'll keep him here at least through tomorrow while he stabilizes. After that, he can complete his recovery at home."

"But it's the weekend. He won't be here by himself, will he?"

"Not for a minute. Either my vet tech or I will be here twenty-four/seven." Julia turned Maddie toward the exit. "Witt, take this girl home now, and make sure she eats something and gets some rest."

"Yes, ma'am." Apparently, Maddie's best friend had decided he could be trusted with that much.

"Wait," Maddie said. "Can't I see him first, at least tell him goodbye?"

Julia exhaled softly. "Of course. He's not awake yet, but I'll take you back."

Witt stayed in the waiting room with Ranger. When Maddie returned, she didn't seem quite as anxious. Witt helped her into the Suburban, and with Ranger in the back seat, they headed home.

By then, it was late afternoon. Maddie looked completely wrung out, so Witt took her to the house and told her to lie down, saying he'd tend to the dogs and horses. "And if you don't mind me snooping around your fridge and pantry, I'll figure out something for supper, too. You just take it easy."

Standing in the middle of the kitchen, she turned and threw her arms around him. "How can I ever thank you, Witt? You're the best thing to happen to me in forever."

For a moment, he was too stunned to think, much less reply. Half his brain was telling him to savor the moment, while the other half was shouting, *Get out of here now, Wittenbauer, or you'll never be able to let her go.*

"Maddie…" He swallowed hard and gently put some distance between them. She looked up at him with sleepy eyes, fatigue the only thing that could explain either her words or the hug. "Go put your feet up. I'll be back after I finish with chores."

Covering a yawn, she nodded and backed toward the living room. When her footsteps faded, Witt somehow managed to get his own feet moving. His chest ached with the pain of missing her arms around him, missing the scent of her hair, missing the sweet if momentary promise of dreams fulfilled.

But could a future with Maddie ever be more than merely a dream? She deserved so much better than a loser like him.

Maddie awoke to the aroma of bacon on the griddle, along with a scent of something sweet and fruity. Stomach rumbling, she rolled toward her nightstand to look at the time. They'd arrived home from the clinic just after four. How had it gotten to be nearly seven o'clock? She must have slept more soundly than she'd thought.

Wisps of a dream floated through her mind… Witt's arms around her, the softness of his faded cotton shirt, the steady beat of his heart beneath her cheek.

Except it wasn't a dream at all. She'd gone to him, right there in the kitchen, and held him as if she couldn't let go. As he'd eased from her embrace, she clearly recalled the look in his shadowed eyes, and the memory both thrilled and terrified her.

"Maddie?" His voice came from the hallway, tentative and soft.

Sitting up, she pushed the tangled curls off her shoulder. "I'm awake."

"I made pancakes and bacon."

The perfect comfort food. A smile worked its way across her lips. "Be right there."

She ran a brush through her hair, then twisted it loosely and secured it with a large butterfly clip. Glimpsing her wrinkled clothes in the mirror, she considered taking time to change, but the supper smells were too enticing. She gave her shirttail a tug, slid her socked feet into a comfy pair of Birkenstocks and ambled to the kitchen.

Witt had just set a steaming pitcher on the table. "I

hope it was okay to use the huckleberry jam I found in the pantry. I added a couple of spoonfuls to the maple syrup while it was warming."

"Mmm, sounds delicious."

"Did you make the jam yourself?" He pulled out her chair, a gentlemanly act she hadn't experienced in a very long time.

"It's from the batch Nana and I made together last summer." A twinge of sadness crept in. "This year will be my first to try it on my own…unless you wanted to help?" She cast him a hopeful smile.

He gave a nervous laugh. "We'll have to see about that."

He stepped around Ranger, who lay stretched out on the floor, and went to the stove to serve up the pancakes and bacon. Returning to the table, he set down their plates and took his seat. As they'd been doing since he'd first suggested it, they recited together the prayer from the embroidered sampler—*Come, Lord Jesus, be our guest. Let these gifts to us be blessed.*

"And Father," Witt added, his head still bowed, "we ask You please to watch over Joey tonight and help him heal quickly and completely. Amen."

"Amen," Maddie whispered over the lump in her throat.

Witt passed her the butter and syrup. When she took her first bite, she couldn't hold back an appreciative groan. "What did you do to these pancakes? They're amazing!"

He winked. "Secret ingredients."

"Well, they can't be too secret if you found them in my pantry. Come on, you have to tell me, because my cheap store-bought pancake mix never tasted this good before, and I know it's not just the huckleberry syrup."

"Okay, it's no big secret, just a little thing my mother used to do." He dabbed a smear of melted butter from the corner of his mouth. "She always added a dash of cinnamon and a teaspoon of vanilla to the batter."

"I'll have to remember that." She dredged another forkful through the syrup and popped it into her mouth. After quickly downing several more bites along with two slices of bacon, she glanced over with an embarrassed grin. "I didn't realize I was so hungry."

"Worry takes it out of you," Witt said with an understanding nod. "It's good you were able to get some rest."

"I think it helped. And this does, too." She gestured with her fork to indicate the meal. "Thank you, Witt. Really. Thank you so much for everything today." Face warming, she cleared her throat. "If I, um…said or did anything…that was…inappropriate…"

"Not at all, Maddie. It's been an emotional day— for both of us," he added under his breath. His chair screeched across the tiles as he shot up. "Could you eat another pancake? There's plenty more."

"Maybe one." She let him serve one onto her plate, though she wasn't sure she could force it down. Did Witt feel it, too, this unexpected shift in their friendship? Or was he only reacting to how she'd let her feelings get away from her this afternoon?

As if Julia were standing next to her, she could hear exactly what her friend would say: *Be careful, Maddie. You've only known this guy a little over a month. You dated Garrett for four years before you discovered his lies.*

"He's not Garrett."

Witt looked up from his second helping of pancakes. "Who's Garrett?"

Oh, no, had she said that out loud? "Someone I used to know. Nobody important."

His mouth quirked. "The look on your face says otherwise."

What would it hurt to tell him, other than reminding her of how mortified she'd been—still was—by her own gullibility? She managed one more bite, then took a sip of water and pushed away from the table. "Garrett was my— He was someone I dated for a few years. We met while he was a visiting professor at the California college where I was teaching."

"What happened?"

"I thought we were in love, that he was getting ready to propose." She looked away. "Until I discovered he already had a wife and three children."

"He was still married?"

"And happily so, apparently." She scoffed. "That may have changed after his wife found out I'd been his out-of-town long-term fling."

Witt shook his head. "Maddie, that's awful. I'm so sorry."

"*I'm* sorry I brought him up in the first place. It's just…" Chewing her lip, she hesitantly met his gaze. "I'm starting to realize Garrett's deception has colored my judgment of every other man who's come into my life, and it needs to stop."

Witt took a moment to let Maddie's words sink in. Her experience with this Garrett person explained a lot about the reservations he'd sensed in her at the beginning of their acquaintance. The fact that she'd so quickly grown to trust him said…what? That she'd learned to cautiously give people the benefit of the doubt?

Or that Angus Nathaniel Wittenbauer was a man worthy to be trusted?

Gnawing on that thought, he stood and began to clear the table. "Stay put. I'll do the dishes."

"No, I want to help." She put away the butter and syrup while he rinsed plates and filled the sink.

With Witt washing and Maddie drying, they fell into a comfortable rhythm. It was pretty much like every other after-meal kitchen cleanup he'd helped with since moving into the barn loft, but tonight it felt different. Less like landlady and tenant, more than a couple of friends sharing chores together. There was a new closeness he couldn't quite describe, a sense of utter *rightness*.

By the time they finished, he knew one thing for certain. He *wanted* to be the kind of man Maddie could trust. The kind of man she could one day think of as much more than a friend.

The kind of man she might just want to spend the rest of her life with.

Chapter Eight

Awake earlier than usual on Sunday morning, Witt didn't wait for Maddie before starting the daily routine. First he fed the horses, mucked their stalls and released them into the paddock. Then he set to work in the kennel. Once the dogs had eaten, he let a few of them out to the play yard while he cleaned their runs.

Maddie arrived as he'd begun with the next group. "You got an early start. Did you leave anything for me to do?"

His pulse quickened at the sight of her. She wore her usual jeans and plaid flannel shirt over a tee, with her mass of strawberry-blond curls secured in a loose ponytail. This morning, though, he gave himself permission to *really* see her, to acknowledge and admire the woman who, day by day, claimed more and more of his heart.

"Witt?" Maddie cocked her head. "You're staring."

"Sorry, my mind was wandering." With a self-conscious laugh, he stepped from the run he'd been spraying out and coiled up the hose. "All done in here. Ranger's keeping an eye on the little guys in the yard. I was about to go check on them. Walk out with me?"

On the way, she said, "I called Julia first thing. She told me Joey had a restful night and is already perking up. He even ate a light breakfast this morning."

"That's great news. Any word on when he can come home?"

"She'll let me know. If he continues improving, possibly later this afternoon." As they reached the gate, she turned to him and sighed. "I'll be calling Alicia Caldwell right after lunch to tell her I'll have to cancel."

"What? No!" He gripped her shoulders. "Maddie, you can't. Think about the money you'll be giving up."

"It was never a sure thing, and anyway, I belong here so I can take care of Joey. Why should I lose an entire day hoping for portrait buyers who may not even materialize?"

He didn't understand. After their informational visit with Alicia, he'd thought she'd begun to get excited about the fair. Sure, she was nervous, but she had the talent. How could she doubt it? How could she not see the potential for increasing both awareness and income for Eventide?

Taking a step back, he fisted his hips. "What are you afraid of, Maddie?"

Her wide-eyed expression said he'd hit a nerve. "I— I'm not." She looked everywhere but at him. "I'm just being practical."

"Practical?" He scoffed. "*Practical* would be *not* missing this chance to raise money to keep the sanctuary running. Isn't that what you want?"

"Of course it is. But I can't be two places at once."

"No, and that's why you have me. Unless..." His mouth firmed. "Unless you don't trust me."

She turned to him, her face crumpling. "I do trust

you, Witt. More than I believed I could ever trust anyone again." Voice breaking, she went on: "All right, I'm
scared. I told you, I don't have my grandmother's gift
for fundraising."

"Maybe not, but you most certainly have her gift for
art. Let your drawings speak for themselves. Let them
speak for Eventide."

Her gaze drifted toward the dogs sniffing around
the yard, and her shoulders rose and fell in a thoughtful sigh. "I know it's what Nana would want."

"Then imagine yourself doing it for her, making her
proud." He drew her into his arms and rested his chin
atop her head. The soft scent of lavender evoked a pleasant flutter in his chest. "Have a little faith, Maddie. See
this through and see what happens."

After a moment, she trembled slightly and straightened. Looking up at him, she asked, "Any chance you
have enough faith for both of us?"

"More than enough. But I'll be praying you find
plenty within yourself."

Rocky scampered over and dropped a dirty tennis
ball at Witt's feet. He picked it up and gave it a toss,
and the little dog chased after it in his bouncy three-
legged trot.

"Now, there's faith for you," Witt said with a chuckle.
"That little guy never gives a thought to what he *can't*
do. He just knows what he wants and goes after it."

No sooner had the words left his mouth than the
truth of them socked him in the gut. What right did
he have telling Maddie to ignore her doubts when he'd
been listening to the can'ts, shouldn'ts and don'ts in his
head for more years than he cared to count? Yeah, he

talked a good line about trusting God and believing in His forgiveness and love. But was he really living it?

You've already admitted what you want, Angus Wittenbauer. It's about time you started accepting your worthiness to receive it. To love and to be loved, not only by God, but by this woman who continually brings out the best in you.

Despite unrelenting misgivings, Maddie agreed not to back out of the fair. The bill for Joey's surgery lay heavy on her mind, so there was no question she could use any extra money her drawings might bring in.

After lunch, she and Witt drove to the church to prepare her booth. The gym looked completely different this afternoon, with row after row of tables and dividers. Dozens of people bustled about hanging drapes and signage, laying tablecloths and setting up displays. A volunteer escorted them to Maddie's location, situated exactly as Alicia Caldwell had promised. From her table, she could look straight down the center aisle to the entrance. Alicia had also left plenty of space within the booth for patrons to pose their pets while Maddie sketched.

Obviously, Alicia and her committee had put a great deal of thought into the layout, because pet-loving shoppers couldn't possibly overlook Maddie's booth. The table on her left displayed an array of fancy pet accessories—bandannas, bows, booties, holiday costumes, even rhinestone-studded collars and leashes. On her right, the vendor was setting out large apothecary jars filled with pet treats in a variety of flavors, some of which Maddie would never have thought of.

Borrowing a stepladder from the person in the next

booth, Witt worked on hanging the banner along the rear wall. In the meantime, Maddie spread Nana's blue gingham tablecloth across the front table, then arranged the drawings Witt had framed. From across the way, her fair neighbors nodded appreciatively.

Alicia came by as they were finishing. "This looks wonderful. I've included your booth in our publicity, so I hope you're prepared for a big turnout."

Maddie cast an uneasy glance toward Witt. "How big, exactly?"

The woman rattled off attendance figures for the past few years. "Judging from advance ticket sales, we're expecting that growth to continue." Beaming a smile, she added, "And comments on our Facebook page indicate a very strong interest in pet portraits."

Maddie could only nod and swallow as Witt enclosed her hand in his reassuring grip.

After finishing at the church, they drove to the clinic to pick up Joey. Wearing a soft, inflatable collar that prevented him from licking his stitches, he greeted Maddie with a happy yip. Seeing him so much perkier took the edge off her worries, at least for now.

Julia followed them out to the car with the dog's meds and post-op instructions. She reminded Maddie she'd meet her in the booth first thing in the morning. "I traded on-call duties with my dad, so I can stay all day."

"That's a relief!" Maddie climbed in back next to Joey on the seat. "And you'll handle all the sales stuff? Because I don't know the first thing about those phone payment apps."

"On top of it—no worries."

That night, Maddie placed Joey's pad and blankets on the floor beside her bed. Witt had offered to take the living room sofa and keep the dog with him and Ranger, but as nervous as Maddie remained about the fair, she'd resigned herself to not getting much sleep anyway.

The next morning, she was up and dressed before six thirty. Witt had insisted he'd cover morning chores, instructing her she was absolutely not to concern herself with anything but the fair. She could at least make him breakfast, though. Whisking a batch of eggs to scramble, she glimpsed him and Ranger striding across to the kennel. Mornings could still be chilly this late in May, and his breath came out in vaporous white puffs.

Such a good man. Good *to* her, and good *for* her.

Estimating about how long it would take him to tend the dogs and horses, she timed the eggs and toast just right. As Witt and Ranger stepped into the kitchen, Joey got up from the blanket she'd spread for him near the pantry and hobbled over, tail wagging.

Giving the old white shepherd a gentle scratch behind the ears, Witt glanced at the table, then frowned at Maddie. "I thought I told you to focus on yourself this morning."

"I woke early and needed to keep busy." Pouring coffee, she arched a brow. "But if you don't want your breakfast, I'm sure Joey and Ranger will enjoy it."

"That'd be a hard no." He yanked out his chair, plopped down and spread a napkin across his thigh.

She snickered and spooned a hearty serving of scrambled eggs onto his plate. Taking a smaller portion for herself, she hoped she could get it down. With the clock ticking toward time to leave, her calm facade wouldn't last much longer.

After breakfast, Witt helped carry her drawing supplies and a small lunch cooler to the Suburban. Alicia had said there'd be a variety of food vendors on-site, but why squander ten dollars or more for a burger and soft drink when she could bring her own meal for a fraction of the cost?

Climbing behind the wheel, she exhaled sharply. "Here goes nothing."

"Would you please stop being such a pessimist? You're gonna do great." Witt reached through the open door to pat her arm. "And don't worry a whit about Joey or the other pups. Ranger and I will take good care of them."

"I know you will. But if anything happens—"

"It won't." He backed away and gently pushed her door closed. Raising his voice as she started the engine, he added, "And try to have fun."

Fun. Right. She'd delivered countless lectures to college classes and successfully conducted group tutoring sessions over Zoom. But in those situations she'd been in her element, doing what she'd studied and trained for—and, frankly, enjoyed.

Not that she didn't enjoy sketching—she loved it, in fact. However, never in a million years had she once imagined drawing for others, much less asking them to pay for it.

She arrived at the church half an hour before the fair opened to the public. Julia was already in the booth, where she'd positioned her iPad with credit card reader next to a cash box, small ledger and receipt book.

"Wow, you thought of everything." Maddie set her things beneath the table, then adjusted the clip holding her hair back. "Did you by chance bring a net for corralling my butterflies?"

"No, but I do have some calming lemon-ginger tea for you." From beside her chair, Julia brought out two travel mugs and passed the yellow one to Maddie.

She took a grateful sip. "And what, dare I ask, is in your mug?"

"Dark roast, extra strong, light on the cream, no sugar. I'm the Caffeine Queen, remember?"

Maddie snickered. "How could I forget?"

Having her best friend to banter with kept her from paying too much attention to the time as they awaited the nine o'clock opening. The noise level gradually rose as more vendors arrived and got organized for the day.

Then, a few minutes before nine, the lady from the pet treat booth came over holding a huge gray Persian tomcat. "Hi, I'm Sarah. Any chance I can beat the rush and have you draw Smokey?"

"Um…okay." Opening one of her new sketchbooks, Maddie invited Sarah to set Smokey on the cloth-draped pedestal she'd arranged inside the booth. "You can stay beside him so he doesn't try to jump off."

The only cats she'd sketched before were the two tabby mousers that lived in the barn, and they hadn't been very cooperative. Smokey, on the other hand, held a regal pose, slitting his eyes as if the whole thing was utterly beneath him. By the time the doors-opening announcement came over the loudspeaker, Maddie had the beginnings of what she deemed a very good likeness. After filling in a few more details and some shading, she had Sarah take a look.

"Oh, you captured his personality perfectly! He looks just like he's saying, 'Don't bother me, lowly human.'" Laughing, she hugged the grumpy-looking cat under her chin. "Let me put Smokey in his crate, and I'll be right back with my credit card."

"First sale," Julia said with a wink. "How does it feel?"

"I think I'm still in shock."

Before Julia finished taking Sarah's payment, two more shoppers approached the table. One held a Chihuahua in a purse-style pet carrier, and the other had a corgi on the end of a bright blue leash. Maddie was soon so busy sketching pets and watching Julia ring up sales that whatever doubts she'd arrived with had vanished. Her new worry became whether she'd brought enough drawing materials to last until closing time.

And her one constant thought was wishing Witt could have been here to witness her success.

Witt wished more than anything that he could have gone with Maddie to the fair. It was past noon already, and he hadn't heard a word from her, which could mean one of two things. Either her booth was a total bust and she regretted letting him persuade her not to cancel, or she was staying too busy to give him a second thought.

He hoped and prayed it was the latter.

With Joey staying in the house for now, Maddie had told Witt to come and go as he pleased. Sitting on the living room floor with Joey and Ranger snoozing on either side of him, he stared at the screen of his cell phone and debated whether to check on Maddie.

Not two seconds later, she called. "I thought you might be waiting for an update."

He wouldn't let on how anxious he'd been. "How's it going?"

"Witt, it's unbelievable!" She sounded breathless. "There's been a steady flow of customers since the doors opened this morning."

"That's great news!" Pumping his fist, he mouthed a silent *Yes!*

"I've had to intentionally slow down a bit so my hand doesn't cramp—and my supplies don't run out."

Joey whimpered softly as he shifted position. Witt gave him a soothing pat to settle him. He'd offer to bring Maddie whatever supplies she needed but knew she wouldn't want him to leave Joey alone.

Then a Scripture passage popped into his head. Closing his eyes, he murmured, "'And the barrel of meal wasted not, neither did the cruse of oil fail, according to the word of the Lord.'"

"From the Bible?"

"First Kings. It's about Elijah and a widow he helped during a severe drought. She never ran out of flour or oil, because the Lord provided enough for each day." His heart warmed with a deep inner assurance. "Just like He'll do for you, today and always."

Maddie grew silent for a moment. "Thank you, Witt." Her voice cracked. "Having you around is helping me find my faith again."

"I doubt it was ever really lost, just a bit neglected."

"Maybe so." She sighed, then changed the subject and asked how Joey was doing.

"Taking it easy. Eating well, lots of naps. He told me to tell you not to worry."

"I know he's in good hands." Voices and a small dog's yip sounded in the background. "Oops, things are picking up again. Gotta go. I'll see you this evening."

Disconnecting, Witt smiled. And not only because of Maddie's successful day so far, but because of the increasing level of trust she'd placed in him. After so many years of *not* being trusted—of being looked upon as a criminal because of his former employment, then bearing the stigma of alcoholism and homelessness—he liked the man he was becoming. His two years at the transitional home had set him on a better path, but with Maddie he'd experienced glimpses of a future he thought he'd lost forever.

It was about time to let the dogs out for a bit. While the kennel dogs roamed and sniffed inside the play yard, he watched Ranger and Joey stretch their legs outside the fence. Leaning on a gate post, he tugged his wallet from his pocket and eased out the faded, ragged-edged photograph he'd managed to hold on to all these years. It was a studio portrait of his son and daughter. Flaxen-haired Emily had been twelve then, and Trent, with darker hair like his dad, had just turned eight. It was the way Witt liked to remember them, while they'd still looked up to him with love and respect.

He doubted he'd ever get past the pain of missing them. But mistakes had consequences, and he was paying the price. Best he could do now was to cling to his faith and keep moving forward.

And today, that meant cooking up a celebratory dinner for Maddie. She was bound to be both exhausted and hungry by the time she got home. The other day in the barn, he'd come across an old charcoal grill and a half-used bag of briquettes. He'd rummaged through her freezer earlier and found some pork chops the perfect size for grilling. Baked potatoes and a green salad would complete the meal.

He tucked the photo back into his wallet. "Let's go, pups. The afternoon's half-gone and we've got stuff to do."

By four o'clock, the crowd began to thin. Back aching, fingers stiff, Maddie stood from the hard metal folding chair to stretch.

"You've made quite the haul today," Julia said as she

perused sales figures on her iPad. "Almost five hundred dollars, and that doesn't count the orders from people who didn't have their pets with them today but are sending you photos."

She released an incredulous chuckle. "Witt and Alicia both tried to tell me. I should have believed them."

"I tried to tell you, too," Julia said with a smirk. "But what does your very best friend know?" She opened a fresh bottle of water and handed it to Maddie—a blessing, because she doubted she'd have had enough grip strength left to open it herself.

After another stretch and a sip of water, Maddie pulled her chair closer. She plopped down and leaned her shoulder into Julia's. "I'll never be able to thank you enough for sticking with me all day. I could never have done this alone."

"It's been fun. Not just watching the money roll in but getting to see you at work." Grinning, Julia cocked her head. "Did you know the tip of your tongue peeks out when you're concentrating on doing a sketch?"

Maddie clamped her lips together. "Um, no. I did not know that."

"It's cute." Julia nodded as a couple strolling by slowed to look at the display of framed drawings. When they'd moved on, she said, "Too bad you didn't have more Eventide brochures for people to pick up."

Maddie had brought all she could scrape together of the ones her grandmother had ordered a few years ago. Those had run out over the noon hour. "They need to be updated, but I've sorely neglected fundraising since Nana died, so getting new brochures printed hasn't been a priority—much less in the budget."

"Well, after today I'd say that's changed. You'll want to have plenty on hand for next time."

She gaped. *"Next time?"*

"Of course. You've found your niche, Maddie. There are all kinds of opportunities like this you could sign up for throughout the year. Just think of all the money you could raise for Eventide."

She couldn't argue the point, but she'd need a few days to assimilate this experience before she could contemplate repeating it.

Glancing up, she noticed a sixtysomething couple hurrying up the aisle, two handsome golden retrievers trotting alongside.

"Oh, good, you're still here." The woman caught her breath as she arrived in front of Maddie's booth. "We were running late and I was afraid we'd miss you. We were hoping to get a portrait of Duke and Duchess."

Maddie rose and invited them behind the table. "Would you like them together or separately?"

"Oh, together, definitely." Lowering her voice to a whisper, the woman said, "They're about to become parents."

Trying not to laugh, Maddie retrieved her pencil and sketchbook while Julia took the couple's information. The Everetts, as with a number of patrons that day, mentioned they'd heard about Maddie's booth from Witt when he'd recently done a handyman job for them.

"He is just the nicest man," Mrs. Everett said as she posed the dogs.

"Hard worker, too," her husband chimed in. "I'd hire him again anytime."

Maddie's heart warmed on behalf of the man she was

coming to care for in ways she couldn't yet explain. "I'll be sure and pass along your compliments."

By the time she finished the portrait, it was nearing five o'clock, and other vendors were beginning to close down their booths. With what little Maddie had brought, it was easy enough to pack up everything while Julia finalized the day's totals. Even minus the cost of supplies and the 25 percent owed to the church, there was no denying it had been an extremely profitable day.

Sighing with pleasure, she furled the banner and placed it in the supplies box. "This would never have happened without Witt."

Julia studied her. "Maddie, are you falling for him?"

"I… I don't know. Maybe I am." Her gaze swept the high gym ceiling. "All I know is, since he came into my life, I'm seeing everything differently. It's like in *The Wizard of Oz*, where Dorothy's life in Kansas is filmed in shades of gray, and then she gets to Oz and everything's in vibrant color."

A concerned smile touched Julia's lips. "Yes, you are definitely falling in love. Just be—"

"You don't have to say it," she interrupted, thrusting out her palm. "I am being careful, I promise. And I'm certainly not ready to use the *L* word yet. But I am sick to death of letting doubt and suspicion control my life. Whether for Witt or someone I have yet to meet, it's time I unbarred the doors of my heart."

Chapter Nine

After the scare with Joey and then the Memorial Day fair, it had taken Maddie most of the week to start sleeping better again and regain her energy. Once again, Witt had picked up the slack by taking over most of the kennel and barn chores and even insisted on cooking a couple of meals.

Although nothing could top those delicious grilled pork chops he'd had waiting for her when she'd gotten home Monday evening.

She had a short break before summer tutoring sessions would begin for students who'd fallen behind during the school year. In the meantime, she couldn't postpone completing the additional orders from the fair. After supplying her with photos of their pets, the patrons had been more than willing to drive out to Eventide to pick up the portraits. Following a brief tour of the sanctuary, many had tacked on sizable donations with their payments.

While cleaning up after breakfast Friday morning, Maddie glanced out the kitchen window as Witt released the horses into the paddock. Reaching through the gate, he offered Sunny and Sage each a peppermint, then braced his forearms across the top rail and gazed into the distance.

She'd noticed a subtle change in him over the past several days. For the most part, he seemed happier, more at peace, even hopeful. Then the light would momentarily fade from those deep-set brown eyes, and she'd glimpse the weight of regret that still lay heavy upon his heart.

Something told her that no matter how far he traveled from those years of homelessness or how much his life improved, he'd never be whole while his children were estranged.

If only she could find them, make them understand how much their father regretted the pain he'd caused, tell them how hard he'd worked to overcome his past and rebuild his life.

Turning away from the window, she massaged her temple. She knew his children's names, and she knew their ages. That should be enough to begin an internet search. Surely as young adults they'd be active on social media. She'd start there. And since Witt would be leaving shortly after eight for what he expected to be an all-day handyman job in Frenchtown, she'd have uninterrupted time at the computer.

Once he and Ranger had climbed into the truck and headed down the lane, she settled at her desk and opened her internet browser—only to be thwarted when neither an Emily nor a Trent Wittenbauer turned up on any of the major social media platforms.

Then it occurred to her that if they really wanted to distance themselves from their father, they could be using a different surname. Possibly their mother's maiden name? Maddie had never heard Witt mention it, so that was a dead end.

Or maybe they'd abbreviated the name, something like... Bauer.

She searched again. This time she found a Facebook account for Trent Bauer. His profile photo looked to be about the right age—nineteen—and there was an unmistakable resemblance to Witt. The About section said he'd grown up in Butte, went to high school in Boise, Idaho, and now attended college at Boise State.

Joey lay by her chair, and she reached down to give him a pat. "What do you think, boy? Have we found Witt's son?"

Trent's privacy settings allowed her to browse his friends list, and among them she found an Emily Bauer Pearson. When she viewed the profile, several photos popped up from Emily's Christmas wedding. One of the photos showed Emily and her groom posing with an attractive ash-blond woman and a balding mustached man. The caption identified the older couple as Emily's mother and stepfather, Linda and Ed Rogers.

Maddie pressed her hand to her heart. "Oh, Witt, your daughter got married and you weren't there to see it."

She wondered if he'd even known about the wedding, but she couldn't ask him without revealing how she'd come across the news. Besides, if he hadn't heard, it wasn't her place to tell him.

However, nothing was stopping her from privately reaching out to Trent and Emily. At worst, they'd tell her to mind her own business and refuse further contact. At best, she could foster a long-overdue reunion between Witt and his children.

Pulse hammering, she opened the message window on Emily's profile page. After thinking hard about what to say, she typed:

Hello, Emily. My name is Maddie McNeill, and I'm a friend of Angus Wittenbauer, who I believe is your father. I don't know all that happened in the past, but I do know he is deeply remorseful for how his actions hurt his family. If only you'd give him a chance to show you he's changed, you'd see for yourself the good man he's become. Please, if you get this, I would so love to arrange for you to see your father again. He loves you and misses you terribly.

. She read through the message several more times, changing a word here and there before taking a deep breath and hitting Send. Then she copied the message and addressed it to Trent. Since she wasn't in their friends list, there was a chance they would never see what she'd sent. She could only pray that one or both of them would check their accounts for message requests and eventually respond...one way or another.

It was all she could do to stop staring at the Messenger window in hopes of seeing a reply come through. Another one of the fair patrons had emailed a pet photo late yesterday requesting a portrait, so she brought the image up on-screen and pulled out her sketchbook and pencils.

She was just finishing when Joey's ears perked up at the sound of Witt's truck in the driveway. Back so soon? He must have forgotten something. Laying her drawing aside, she checked once more for a response to her messages—nothing yet—then made sure to close her internet browser in case Witt ventured into the study.

Minutes later, he rapped on the back door, then called to her from the mudroom. Always the gentlemen, he never stepped beyond the threshold without being invited.

"Come on in, Witt." Striding through the living room, she strove for a nonchalant smile. "I thought you'd be gone for hours yet."

"Turned out to be a simple fix after all." He shuffled from one foot to the other, his fiftysomething features looking suddenly boyish. "Since I've got the afternoon free now, I, uh…wondered if you'd like to—I mean, uh…"

Her heart thudded. Was he trying to ask her for a *date*? "What…um…" Great. Now *she* was stammering. She cleared her throat. "What did you have in mind?"

"Nothing in particular." Releasing an embarrassed laugh, he shrugged. "I just thought it would be nice to get outside and enjoy this sunny day—" he glanced away briefly, then met her gaze "—together."

It was the sweetest invitation she'd had in forever. Softly she replied, "I'd like that very much." Then an idea came to her. She wiggled her brows. "Any chance I could interest you in a horseback ride?"

He looked at her like she'd just suggested they jump off a speeding train from a hundred-foot-high trestle into a river teeming with piranhas.

She laughed out loud. "Witt. Don't tell me you've never been on a horse."

"I've never been on a horse." He gulped. "I like horses just fine. As long as I'm standing on solid ground with no flying hooves or bared teeth involved."

"Then you already know Sunny and Sage are perfectly safe. They're the gentlest horses this side of the Rockies." She set a finger to her chin. "What if I make sandwiches? We can ride up the hill to my favorite spot and have a picnic lunch."

"I don't know…" He waved one hand as he backed toward the door, then almost tripped as Ranger blocked his escape. He glared at the dog. "Whose side are you on?"

With a smirk, Maddie turned to the refrigerator to grab some sandwich fixings.

Half an hour later, she secured their picnic lunch behind Sunny's saddle, then marched around to tighten Sage's cinch. Arms crossed, Witt watched from a safe distance.

She motioned him closer. "Come on, it'll be fun."

"No trotting, galloping or rearing?"

"No worries. We'll keep the pace slow and steady so Joey can come along for a little exercise, too."

It took several more reassurances before she coaxed him onto Sage. Mounted on Sunny, she led the way across the meadow, while Ranger and Joey followed along with occasional side trips to sniff out something in the grass.

After a while, Maddie looked over at Witt to find him smiling. The tension had left his shoulders, and he no longer clutched the saddle horn in a death grip.

She grinned. "Look at you, cowboy."

"This is actually kind of nice." He gave the buckskin's neck a pat, and as he exhaled slowly, his expression turned wistful. "Emily took riding lessons for a while. Linda always took her, though. I was spending too many hours at the office back then." Jaw clenched, he added under his breath, "Another mistake I'll regret for the rest of my life."

She nudged Sunny closer, until her knee brushed

Witt's and she could touch his arm. "You've got to stop beating yourself up over the past. Things are going to get better, Witt. You've made me believe it. Now you should, too."

His eyes locked on hers, and his winsome smile returned. "Things are already better…thanks to you."

Pulse racing, throat tight, she could hardly swallow. "I…um…"

Her cell phone chimed with the tone for an incoming Facebook message. She didn't think her heart could beat any faster, but it did. Excusing herself, she put a bit of distance between them and tugged her phone from her pocket. Holding it so Witt couldn't accidentally see the screen, she read the message.

Yes, I'm Angus Wittenbauer's daughter. I can't believe you found me. It's been a long time, and there's so much I need to tell him. Maybe you could arrange for us to meet somewhere?

"Everything okay?" Witt asked.

"Oh. Yes. Fine." Her face must be a dozen shades of red. "Just something I need to take care of later." She spied her favorite picnic spot a little farther up the hill. "I'm getting hungry. Let's have our lunch under that tall cottonwood."

Although, with the nervous excitement coursing through her, she'd be doing well to swallow a single bite.

A relaxing afternoon with Maddie? What more could Witt have asked for? He hadn't expected to find himself on horseback, but that had turned out okay, too. Add a picnic beneath a towering cottonwood tree, an early-summer breeze humming through the branches and an expansive view of the greening countryside spread before them...the day had been just about perfect.

He only wished he knew what had diverted Maddie's attention for most of the afternoon. Although he thought she'd enjoyed their outing as much as he had, ever since that message had come in on her phone, she'd been distracted. Not worried, exactly, but definitely preoccupied. And maybe a tiny bit giddy?

If it had been news about Joey's lab results, she would have told him. She had to know he was equally anxious about the old dog's prognosis. And she'd been so open with him about other aspects of her life. What was it she didn't feel she could tell him now?

Or maybe you two aren't getting as close as you'd like to hope?

He didn't really believe that, either, not the way things had been between them lately. He just needed to trust that if it was something important, she'd tell him when she felt ready.

That evening, after they'd completed chores and were sitting down to supper, Maddie's house phone rang. She crossed to the counter to pick up the extension. Reading the caller ID, she clutched her stomach. "It's Julia."

When she let the phone continue to ring, Witt got up and took it from her. "Let me," he said gently, then answered.

"Witt?" The veterinarian sounded confused. "I was trying to reach Maddie. I have Joey's results."

"She's right here. But she's a little too shaky to talk."

"Well, you can tell her Joey's mass was benign. No further treatment necessary."

When he squeezed Maddie's hand and mouthed the

word *benign*, she sank to the floor and tearfully called the big white dog into her arms.

"Thank you, Dr. Frasier. She's relieved beyond words." Witt laughed as Joey showered Maddie's face with doggy kisses and Ranger tried to get in on the act. "We all are."

"Me, too. Joey's a very special dog. I'm headed home to put my feet up, so tell Maddie I'll talk to her tomorrow. And by the way," she added, her tone mellowing, "my friends call me Julia."

Witt's chest warmed. So he'd won over Maddie's hypervigilant protector. That had to be a good sign.

As he returned the phone to its base, Maddie pushed to her feet and threw her arms around him. "Thank the Lord! Thank *you*!"

Gasping, he fought to regain his balance before they both toppled over. Maybe it was merely her spontaneous reaction to the good news, but nothing in recent memory compared to the physical and emotional delight of holding her in this moment of celebration. When she tilted her head to smile up at him, thoughts of Joey flew from his mind, and all he could think about was kissing her.

Heart thumping, he drew a breath and leaned closer. "Maddie…"

She pressed her palms against his chest and croaked out a weak laugh. "Oh, dear, I almost forgot about supper. We should eat before it gets any colder."

"Right." Reluctantly, he dropped his arms to his sides. "Cold mac 'n' cheese is the worst."

But as they sat down to the meal, her trembling hands and shallow breaths told him she'd been as deeply affected by his almost-kiss as he'd been.

Someday, Maddie McNeill. I'm praying that someday you'll trust me completely.

On Saturday, things seemed mostly back to normal between them, although he detected some residual awkwardness after last night's moment of closeness.

He also couldn't shake the feeling that she had something entirely different on her mind. With her success at the fair and then the orders she'd received afterward, he didn't think it was financial issues. And the way she'd been glued to her cell phone since yesterday, as if continually checking for messages...

As he turned over the soil in Maddie's vegetable garden, a new possibility socked him in the gut. *Was there someone else?* Maybe she'd never given up on the lying two-timer she'd been in love with before. Maybe she'd just been biding her time until he left his wife and was free to marry her. Maybe...

When Maddie touched his arm, he nearly jumped out of his skin.

She hopped out of the way before the shovel he'd been using hit her foot. "Witt, are you okay?"

"You startled me, that's all."

"Sorry. But before that, you looked upset. Even angry."

Retrieving the shovel, he tried to laugh off her concern. "I'm mad at myself for putting this off so long. The *Farmers' Almanac* says it's past time for planting summer vegetables."

She frowned and narrowed one eye. "Since when are you reading the *Farmers' Almanac*?"

"Since you said something a couple of weeks ago about getting the garden ready for beans and squash and...whatever. I figured I ought to educate myself, so I picked up a copy in town the other day."

Her eyes fell shut briefly as a tiny smile puckered her lips. He had the distinct feeling she was trying not to laugh. "Well, thank you," she said. "I'm heading to the market for groceries. I'll pick up some bedding plants at the Elk Valley Garden Center next door. Need anything else while I'm—"

A chime sounded from her jeans pocket. She pulled out her phone, gnawing her lip as she read another text.

Witt leaned on the shovel and tried to sound casual as he asked, "Anything important?"

"It's the lady I did a pet portrait for yesterday. She wants to come out later this afternoon to get it." She was already thumb-typing a reply. "I told her I have some errands to run and should be home by three o'clock."

He wanted to kick himself. All these messages lately—probably just her portrait customers checking in. As busy as they'd kept her, no wonder she'd been preoccupied. He was agonizing over nothing.

"Oh, before I go," she said, "have you made any Sunday plans yet?"

"Uh, no. Just church in the morning and a restful afternoon."

"You've been attending Elk Valley Community of Faith, haven't you?"

"Most Sundays, yes." Where was she going with this? Maybe thinking about returning to church, herself? "The people have been very welcoming, and the preacher always gets me looking at Scripture with fresh eyes."

Glancing away, Maddie murmured, "I remember that about Pastor Peters." She inhaled deeply, all business again. "So. Tomorrow. What if we attend church together and then drive over to Frenchtown for lunch? There's a little café where I meet Julia every once in a while. I think you'd like it."

True, he'd only known her for several weeks, but this invitation seemed about as incongruous with Maddie McNeill's character as horseback riding yesterday had been for him. Did recent events signify promising changes in their relationship…or should he be more worried than ever?

"Witt?" Her lips twitched in a hesitant smile. When she tilted her head, strands of strawberry-blond waves fell across one eye. "Is that okay?"

He drew a hand down his face. "Uh, sure. Church and lunch tomorrow. Sounds good."

Leaving Joey to loll in a sunny patch of grass with Ranger, Maddie left on her errands, and Witt got back to work on the garden plot. He needed the distraction of physical labor to keep from dwelling too much on Maddie's departure from the ordinary. Not that he wasn't delighted that she wanted to attend worship with him—hadn't he been praying for exactly that?

Maybe it was just nerves on his part. He was fifty-one years old, for crying out loud. He'd married his college sweetheart, and after Linda, there'd never been anyone else. As if any woman would have wanted him during those dark years.

Nope, this was all new territory, and he wasn't navigating it very well.

He knocked off work a little before three and went to the loft to wash off several layers of garden soil. When he came down later with Ranger and Joey, he found Maddie showing a thirtysomething couple and two young children around the kennel. The kids immediately ran over to pet the dogs.

The girl and boy reminded Witt so much of Emily and Trent at those ages that he could hardly breathe. Hand to his heart, he backed toward the door. Would there ever come a time when he'd finally forgive himself for the years he'd missed of his children's lives?

Maddie's eyes softened with a look that said she'd read his thoughts. "Mr. and Mrs. Harvey, I'd like you to meet Witt. He's my right-hand man around here. And those two special dogs are Ranger and Joey." She proceeded to tell the story of Witt and Ranger's reunion, tactfully omitting the part about Witt's homeless years and saying only that they'd gotten separated when Witt had taken seriously ill.

The conversation gave Witt time to collect himself—and also to appreciate how naturally Maddie had segued into talking more about Eventide's mission. By the time the family left with their dog's portrait, the Harveys had promised Maddie a monthly donation to help fund the sanctuary.

As they watched them drive away, Witt gave a snort. "I better not ever hear you say again how bad you are at schmoozing and fundraising."

A blush crept up Maddie's cheeks. "I didn't fully understand until now that it's really just about sharing my passion." She linked her arm through his and rested her head on his shoulder. "Thank you, Witt, for cracking open my shell and nudging me out of my comfortable, quiet existence."

He suppressed a shuddering breath, but he couldn't keep a smile from spreading across his face. Whatever doubts and misgivings still nagged at him, Maddie had a way of making him feel valued, appreciated, worthy. If, someday, she could see him as a man she could love, could willingly spend the rest of her life with, he'd never ask God for another thing.

Chapter Ten

Maddie was a nervous wreck. After so many months away from church, she anticipated some discomfort when she first stepped through those doors. On the other hand, she regularly ran into these people around Elk Valley, and most knew how she'd struggled after Nana passed away. Pastor Peters had stayed in touch, too, although the frequency of his calls had lessened over time—no doubt due to her increasingly evasive responses. She must apologize for that. And thank him for not giving up on her.

Choosing what to wear, she paired an aqua lace-trimmed top with a floral-print calf-length skirt she'd had for years. Jeans, flannel and cotton T-shirts had been her go-to attire for so long that it felt strange to be this dressed up. This morning would also be the first time since Joey's surgery she was leaving him home alone. Witt never went anywhere without Ranger, even to church, where he said everyone had accepted the dog as his emotional support animal. Maddie couldn't exactly claim the same about Joey, but thankfully he seemed happy to return to the kennel, wagging his tail as he greeted his doggy friends before trotting into his run.

Actually, the greatest source of Maddie's nerves today was what came *after* church. Emily Bauer Pearson had agreed to meet them for lunch, and Maddie was praying with every fiber of her being that Witt's reunion with his daughter would bring much-needed healing for both of them.

She let Witt drive them to church in the Suburban and tried to keep her knees from bouncing as she gazed out the passenger-side window.

Pulling up outside the steepled white building, Witt reached over to pat her arm. "Take it easy. This can't be any scarier than doing the arts and crafts fair."

"It's not that. I…um…" She yanked open her door. "Let's just go inside." As Witt got out and clipped a leash on Ranger, she wished she'd brought Joey along after all, because today she could use all the emotional support she could get.

Judging from the number of greetings Witt received on their way inside, it appeared he'd already made many friends here. Despite having grown up attending Elk Valley Community of Faith with her grandparents, Maddie was the one who felt like a newcomer.

They scooted into a pew near the back as the music leader opened the service with a melodic call to worship. The blend of familiar old hymns and contemporary praise songs, then Pastor Peters's insightful message about the healing power of forgiveness, reached deep into Maddie's heart. Midway through the sermon, she became aware of the tears coursing down her cheeks. She hadn't realized how she'd been stuffing away her anger and unforgiveness over Garrett's duplicity, and also toward the corrupt investment company that had stolen not only her grandparents' life savings but their health—their very lives—as well.

Perhaps even worse, she'd failed to acknowledge how such bitterness had kept her from living her own best life.

"And we have God's firm assurance," the pastor concluded, "that He is able to replace sorrow with joy, despair with hope, shame with forgiveness, hostility with love. 'O taste and see that the Lord is good: Blessed is the man that trusteth in him.'"

As they stood for the closing hymn, Witt slid his arm around her, a shelter amidst the storm of her emotions. "You okay?"

She nodded and blew her nose into a tissue. "I needed this more than I knew."

Eyes lifted toward the cross above the altar, he sighed. "Show me one person on this earth who doesn't."

They waited in the pew while other congregants filed out, several stopping to say hello and welcome Maddie back. Then Pastor Peters approached. After shaking Witt's hand, he reached past him for Maddie's and smiled warmly. "It's real good to see you again. We've missed you."

More collected now, she tipped her head toward Witt. "You can thank this guy. He's been after me to come to church with him for weeks."

"Well, good for you, Witt." The pastor clapped him on the shoulder, then winked at Maddie. "Seems the Lord bringing you two together has been a blessing for you both. Not to mention this handsome fella," he added, giving Ranger a pat.

Tingles raced up Maddie's spine. "I agree."

On their way out, a few of Maddie's acquaintances caught her to say they'd heard about her booth at the Memorial Day fair. For various reasons, they hadn't been able to make it that day, but wondered if she could still do portraits of their pets.

"Of course, of course," she assured them. "Call me and we can set something up."

In the car, Witt looked over at her with a hopeful grin. "Are you glad you came?"

"I am. Thank you."

"You give me too much credit." He started the engine. "You'd have found your way back in the Lord's good time."

She no longer doubted he was right. She was also more certain than ever that God's perfect timing had everything to do with Witt's arrival at the sanctuary exactly when she'd needed him in her life.

Now if only God would make sure Emily showed up as promised, because Maddie had to believe she'd never have been able to find Witt's children—much less arrange this meeting—if it hadn't also been part of God's plan.

They'd reached I-90, and Witt steered the Suburban up the eastbound entrance ramp. "So where's this café we're going to?"

"Take the Frenchtown exit and I'll direct you from there."

Nodding, he glanced over at Maddie. Her knees were jumping again, maybe even worse than before. Church had gone fine. How could she still be so antsy? Was it the idea of dining with him in a public place, like they were an actual couple?

He was a little nervous about it, himself. She'd issued the invitation, but should he ask for separate checks, or should he offer to pay for both their meals? What was the protocol here?

Tense silence ensued, neither of them speaking again until they came into Frenchtown. As Witt exited onto the feeder road, Maddie told him to take the next right. After a couple more turns, they arrived at a long cabin-like building with a nearly full parking lot. The sign at the road read *Smith Family Hometown Café—bring your appetite and stay awhile!*

Witt wasn't sure he could eat a thing.

While he drove through the lot looking for an empty parking spot, it occurred to him he should have dropped Ranger off at home. "See anywhere with some shade? I didn't think about having to leave Ranger in the car."

Maddie shook herself as if gathering her thoughts. "Not a problem. They have pet-friendly outdoor dining. That's why I chose this place."

As they continued around to the rear of the café, Witt glimpsed a covered deck that ran the length of the building. He breathed a little easier when he spotted more than a few leashed dogs of various sizes sitting or lying near their owners' chairs. Leave it to Maddie to think of everything.

After another trip around the building, he found a vacant spot and pulled in. Maddie hopped out of the car before he could make it around to get her door. He clipped on Ranger's leash and followed her to the open-air seating, where they were greeted by a hostess.

"Table for two?" The ponytailed teen in black jeans beamed a toothy smile.

Maddie stepped closer to the hostess and said something Witt couldn't hear. The girl checked the seating diagram on her podium, then grabbed menus and a handful of napkin-wrapped tableware—at least three sets, by Witt's count. Who else was Maddie expecting?

Following the hostess to their table, he tried to keep Ranger from sniffing every plate and every other dog's rear end. Good thing most diners—and dogs—took his curiosity in stride.

"Here you go," the hostess said. "Away from the crowd, like you asked." She laid out the menus and tableware. "Shall I send over three waters?"

"Yes, thanks. And a water bowl for the dog, please." With a tentative smile at Witt, Maddie took her seat.

Growing more uneasy by the minute, he lowered himself into the chair on her left and told Ranger to lie down. He nodded toward the empty seat across from him. "Want to tell me who the other menu's for? Because I'm pretty sure Ranger can't read."

Her expression softened, and she reached for his hand. "I'm sorry for all the secrecy, but I wanted it to be a surprise. I wasn't even sure I could make it happen until I worked out the details yesterday."

He wrinkled his brow. "All those messages you were getting on your phone?"

"Most of them, yes." She glanced over her shoulder, then back at Witt. "I wanted to do something special for you, and I thought…"

Still confused, he glimpsed a young woman weaving through the tables and coming their way. The shape of her face, the ash-blond hair… He felt like he should recognize her.

And then he did.

His throat closed. He shoved up from his chair, a whispered name scraping across his dry lips. "Emily."

"Hello, Dad." Her tight expression held not an ounce of warmth.

Maddie was standing now, too. "I'm so glad you could make it, Emily. I'll give you two a few minutes—"

"No need. And I won't be staying." Her merciless gaze raked across Witt like the tines of a pitchfork. "But I couldn't pass up the opportunity to look my father in the eye and tell him exactly how much I hate him."

Maddie gasped. Witt could do nothing but stand rooted to the floor and try to bear up under the mountain of hurt and anger his daughter had come to release.

He extended one hand in a gesture of submission. "Whatever you need to say, Emily, I deserve it. But please don't take it out on Maddie. She's been a good friend to me. She was only trying to help."

Chin lifted, Emily glared. "So how much have you told her, exactly? Does she know what you did? How you betrayed us? How you disgraced and destroyed our family?"

Ranger was on his feet now, his obsidian eyes fixed on Emily and his body pressed against Witt's leg. A low growl rumbled in his throat.

"Easy, boy. It's okay." Witt rested his hand on the dog's head and drew a steadying breath.

Before he could find his next words, Maddie spoke up. "Yes, Emily, I know enough." Her smile cordial but insistent, she continued softly, "And now I'd like you to sit down and stop making a scene."

The girl's eyes widened. Whether it was Maddie's schoolteacher tone or finally registering the embarrassment of a public display, Emily quietly pulled out her chair and sat.

"Thank you," Maddie said, taking her own seat. She stared at Witt until he did the same. "Now, can we start over, please?"

There was an awkward silence while the server brought a carafe of ice water, glasses and a bowl for Ranger. Maddie politely told him they weren't yet ready to order. Witt wasn't sure he'd ever be.

The server left, and Maddie filled their water glasses, then poured the rest into Ranger's bowl. While the dog lapped noisily, Witt took a long swig to soothe his parched throat.

Emily sat stiffly, arms crossed, her stony gaze fixed on something beyond Witt's shoulder. "If you're waiting for me to say I forgive you, we'll be sitting here a long time."

The sunlight's shifting rays made something sparkle on Emily's left hand. Witt's heart stopped. "You're... *married*?"

She nodded. "Since Christmas. To an upstanding, hardworking, devoted man," she added pointedly.

"I... I'm happy for you." He meant it, truly, but he could barely get the words past the lump in his throat. How could he not have known his only daughter had fallen in love and gotten married?

Beneath the table, Maddie touched his knee, empathy filling her gaze. She turned to Emily. "I suspect your mother would have used those same words to describe your father in their early years of marriage. Am I wrong?"

Emily's jaw trembled. "No, I suppose not."

"But things happen that even the happiest families

would never have predicted or imagined," Maddie said. "Good people sometimes make horrible mistakes— mistakes they will regret for the rest of their lives. And no matter how badly they wish they could change the past, all they can control is who they are today. So even though I haven't known your dad for very long, I believe I know his heart, and this is not the same man who hurt you so deeply."

Eyes welling, Witt could barely comprehend such loyalty, such confidence in his character. He looked from Maddie to his daughter, hoping to see something in Emily's face that said Maddie's words had penetrated—some hint that she might someday find it in her heart, if not to forgive him, at least not to despise him.

He extended his hand across the table, beckoning her to take it, doubting she would. "My sweet baby girl. I can't undo the past—the dear Lord knows how I wish I could. I have both longed for and dreaded the day I'd see you again, and now that you're here—" He choked back a sob and hoped he wouldn't completely break down in front of everyone at the café. "Now that you're here," he went on with slightly more control, "I just want to know everything about you. Have you been well? Are you happy? Do you stay in touch with Trent?"

"Dad…" Her hand inched toward his before she abruptly drew it into her lap. "Yes, I'm happy. I'm a kindergarten teacher now."

"That's wonderful." Witt sniffed. "I can still see you trying to talk your little brother into playing school when you were kids."

Her brows lifted briefly as if surprised he remembered. "Trent's a sophomore at Boise State. He's majoring in kinesiology. And yes, he still plays piano."

His children were okay—that was all that mattered. "I'm so proud of you both."

"No thanks to you." The iciness in her tone had returned. She scooted her chair back. "It was hard at first, but Mom and Trent and I—we got past the humiliation and rebuilt our lives. And maybe you *have* changed— I don't know. But we've survived without you for this long, so why risk being hurt again?" Rising, she hiked her chin. "Nope, I'm done. And don't bother reaching out to Trent, because he doesn't need you either. Goodbye."

He could do nothing but watch his daughter walk away, and with her, the last fragile shards of hope that he could ever again have a place in his children's lives.

Maddie gripped the arms of her chair. She couldn't bring herself to look at Witt—couldn't bear to see his heartbreak, his despair, his utter devastation.

What have I done?

Everything in her wanted to chase after Emily and beg her to come back to the table, to really talk to her father, to give him a chance to convince her he was a different man. But people were already staring and whispering, uncomfortably aware of the private drama playing out in this public setting.

Would Witt ever forgive her for this?

When she did finally look his way, she found him calmly perusing the menu. If she hadn't already memorized every nuance of his expression—the different ways his eyes crinkled at the corners when something either amused or worried him, or how his mouth quirked to the left when he was concentrating—she might have remained unaware of the pain he tried so hard to hide.

"Witt—"

"We should order something before the manager kicks us out." His Adam's apple worked. "I'm thinking the patty melt. How about you?"

"Witt, you don't have to do this. We can go." Clutching her purse, she edged away from the table.

He stopped her, his eyes locking on hers. "You tried, Maddie. It's okay. *I'm* okay."

"But I'm not." Her voice shook. "I'm so sorry. I should have minded my own business. I should never have—"

"Maddie. Stop." He cupped her cheek, his thumb brushing away an escaping tear. "When I saw my daughter coming this way, when I realized why you'd brought us here, I let myself hope. But it's too late, and I've got to accept it. My children have their lives, and I..." His gaze overflowed with such tenderness that her breath caught. "I have mine. Right here. Right now. With you."

Everything she wanted to say to this man lodged in her throat. Pressing deeper into his palm, she covered his hand with her own and hoped he'd see in her eyes how much she'd grown to care for him.

A quiet cough announced someone else's presence. "Sorry to interrupt." The young man's name tag read *James, Manager.* "There seemed to be a problem earlier. Is there anything I can do to help?"

Maddie straightened and attempted a smile. "Thank you, but...um..."

"We were having some family issues," Witt supplied. "Apologies for the disturbance. I think we'd like to order now."

By the time their food arrived, most of the attention

had died down. Somehow—Maddie wasn't sure how—they managed to finish most of the meals they'd ordered. Ranger savored the last bites of Witt's patty melt and a few slivers of meat from Maddie's chicken Caesar salad. Maddie insisted on paying the bill, and afterward, they slipped out a side exit and headed to the Suburban.

The ride back to Elk Valley was a quiet one. Maddie wished Witt would say something—anything. Every now and then he'd reach over and pat her hand, as if she were the one who'd just had her heart shredded, stomped on and tossed in the dung heap. True, she was doing plenty of sniffling. Witt may have already forgiven her, but she'd never forgive herself for her part in such a cruel disappointment.

At home, he parked the Suburban in the carport, then let Ranger out of the back seat. "I'll go check on the kennel dogs and let them out for some playtime," he said as Maddie joined him on the driveway. "Do you want Joey to come to the house afterward?"

"No, I think he's happier with his friends." She cast him a hopeful smile. "But if you'd like to come in later, we could play cribbage or watch a movie on TV or something."

"Thanks, but I'm pretty tired. Think I'll spend a restful afternoon in the loft."

Seizing his hand, she studied him. "Are you sure that's a good idea?"

"I really am okay, Maddie." Eyes shining, he lifted her hand to his lips. "In fact, I think what happened today was a good thing."

She grimaced. "How can you say that? Witt, I messed up so badly."

"It's good because seeing Emily again made me realize I can finally let go. All these years I've been tormented by the damage I'd caused my kids, but today I know they made it through. They survived in spite of me, and I can rest easy now."

Rest easy? What did he mean by that? Heart hammering, throat clenched, she gripped his wrists. "Witt, promise me—"

He laughed softly and drew her into his arms. "I promise you that I will be down for evening chores and supper as usual, and tomorrow, too, and every day thereafter. I am not going anywhere, Maddie McNeill, unless you send me away."

Reassured, she sank deeper into his embrace. As the fresh, woodsy scent of soap and aftershave filled her senses, her anger toward Emily melted into pity. How was it possible that anyone could ever doubt Witt's goodness and integrity? How could anyone not see that his heart was as big and broad and beautiful as the whole state of Montana?

Chapter Eleven

It took the passage of time along with great effort, but Witt was determined not to allow Emily's rejection to snatch away the happiness he'd found here at Eventide.

The happiness he'd found with Maddie.

Their friendship deepened daily but with a tacit agreement to take things slowly. For Witt's part, he needed to believe he had something tangible to bring to a relationship—something besides hard work and a willing heart. He was living over Maddie's barn, eating at her table, often driving her vehicle whenever they went anywhere together. His earnings as a handyman, while fairly steady, would hardly support a wife the way he thought he should—and wanted to—even knowing none of that would matter to Maddie.

Besides, he wasn't sure she was ready to think of them as…whatever they called seriously dating couples these days. He hadn't even kissed her yet, though as the weeks passed, there'd been more than a few almosts. He cherished the moments of connection when they'd hold hands during an evening walk or admire a sunrise together before tending the kennel dogs, moments when he'd glimpse a yearning warmth in her turquoise eyes. But before he could find the courage to touch his lips to hers, she'd widen the space between them and casually divert his attention. It seemed as if she couldn't escape the memory of being hurt before.

Then he'd seethe inside and imagine himself throttling the man who'd toyed so carelessly with Maddie's affections. She was too beautiful, too kind, too amazingly wonderful to be this hesitant to let love in.

And all the more reason she deserved better than Witt could offer.

He'd told himself a million times he needed to stop thinking like that. God already saw him as worthy, had made him worthy through Jesus's sacrifice on the cross. But old thought patterns were hard to break, and he prayed every day that both Maddie and he would one day shake free of the destructive effects of their pasts.

One Saturday morning in mid-August, while they scooped dog food and meted out meds and supplements, Maddie nudged Witt's arm. "I think we deserve a day off. Are you with me?"

He had to admit, they'd both stayed pretty busy all summer. Word-of-mouth referrals had kept Witt flush with handyman jobs, a good thing because he was slowly building up his savings. Maddie had secured booth space at a few more events in and around Missoula, with another big one coming up on Labor Day weekend. Her pet portraits continued to generate substantial income for the sanctuary, both in sales and extra donations.

He dropped two chewable joint treats into Rocky's bowl. "What did you have in mind?"

"I thought we could drive up the mountain to look for huckleberry patches while the picking's still good."

Just thinking about the deliciously tart sweetness of Maddie's homemade huckleberry jam made his mouth water. "Soon as we're done here, I'll get the berry buckets."

The nearly cloudless sky and warm summer breeze made it a perfect day for an outing. Maddie decided to bring Joey along, which was perfectly fine with Ranger since the dogs had become best buds over the summer. With the two dogs in the back seat of the Suburban and Witt behind the wheel, they headed north from Elk Valley up a winding mountain road.

The temperature dropped incrementally as they climbed. The dogs poked their snouts out the open back windows, ears flapping and tongues lapping up the fresh, pine-scented air. When Witt leaned his head out his window and mimicked the dogs, Maddie burst out laughing. The pure sound of it lit a flame in Witt's chest.

A little farther up, Maddie pointed ahead. "There's a patch that doesn't look too picked over. Let's stop."

Filling a bucket with huckleberries wasn't exactly fast work, and it didn't help that for every ten berries they picked, they ate at least one or two…or more. Witt sighed with pleasure each time he popped one of the tiny, dark purple berries into his mouth and let the tangy flavor explode across his tongue.

He looked across a bush to see Maddie grinning at him. "You're eating my profits," she said. "I'd thought about taking several jars of jam to the Labor Day festival to sell at my booth."

"Oops."

"It's okay. This close to the end of berry season, I doubt we'll gather enough to make it worthwhile."

"Just let me know if you plan on selling the jam you made a couple of weeks ago, because I'll save you the trouble and buy the whole batch."

She stood close enough to give him a playful slap on the arm and almost made him drop his bucket of berries. He yelped and grabbed his bicep as if she'd really hurt him, then tried to tug her ponytail before she ducked out of reach. With both dogs wanting to get in on the fun and nearly tripping them, soon they were laughing so hard that they had to set down their buckets before they spilled every berry they'd gathered.

Witt wasn't sure how it happened, but somehow Maddie ended up in his arms. Their laughter died away, and when she gazed up at him, invitation in her eyes, he couldn't stop himself from kissing her.

It was everything he'd imagined, everything he'd longed for. Fingers tangled in her curls, he cradled her head.

She pressed her forehead against his chest. When she drew a shaky breath, he was pretty sure she was smiling.

Drawing her closer, he fought to get his pulse and breathing under control. "It's been a long, long time since I kissed a beautiful woman. I hope it was okay."

"It's been a long time since I've been kissed." She tilted her head until their eyes met, her languid smile fully visible now. "But I can assure you, that was much better than okay."

He tried to swallow, but there wasn't a drop of moisture left in his mouth. Gently but firmly, he eased her away. "Maybe we should head back."

"Good idea." Her voice sounded almost as raspy as

his. She bent to retrieve their buckets. "Looks like just enough for a pie," she said brightly. "If I get started right after lunch, it'll be cool enough to eat by suppertime."

Witt considered offering to help—nothing he'd like better than spending the rest of this gorgeous day at Maddie's side—but he decided a wiser use of his time would be to make a little more progress on the barn and kennel repairs he wanted to finish before the first winter snows blew in. The calendar might say August, but as fall approached, Montana weather could take some surprisingly harsh turns.

The thought reminded him of the nasty spring snowstorm that had brought Maddie into his life. Sometimes it could take a while, but he'd learned over the years that with a little patience and a whole lot of faith, God had a knack for bringing incredible and undeserved blessings out of the worst imaginable situations.

"Good job on the punctuation worksheet, Eva." Maddie smiled at the ninth grader's image in the Zoom window. "We'll review parts of speech on Thursday so you'll be ready for your English quiz next week."

"Thanks, Ms. McNeill. You're so good at making this grammar stuff make sense."

"You're welcome. See you in a couple of days." Ending the session, she sighed. If only someone could make financial stuff make sense for her.

As portrait sales and sanctuary donations had steadily increased over the summer, Witt remained unwavering in his support. But whenever she sought his thoughts on how best to handle this newfound revenue, it was like a curtain fell across his eyes.

And oh, those eyes! She could get lost in them—and

almost had, more than once. Then that kiss on Saturday, and she was undone. How in the world could she have reached forty-six years old with two new gray hairs as of this week and still tremble like a lovesick teenager at the mere thought of being in Witt's arms?

Maybe because you really are falling in love?

"Knock, knock!"

At the sound of Witt's singsong call from the mudroom, she nearly fell off her desk chair. Self-consciously tucking a curl behind her ear, she hoped her face wouldn't give away the recent direction of her thoughts. "Be right there."

Holding a stack of mail, he waited just across the threshold. "The mail truck was pulling up when I got home an hour ago, but I didn't want to interrupt your tutoring session."

"All done for the day." She crossed the kitchen and held out her hand. "Let's see what we've got."

A funny smile on his face, he passed her the stack. "It's a hot one out there. Mind if I get a glass of ice water?"

"Angus Wittenbauer." She rolled her eyes. "You do not need a special invitation to help yourself to anything in my kitchen."

While he filled a glass, she plopped down at the table to sort through the mail. Bills, ads…and a letter from the Missoula pet supply store that a few months ago had withdrawn their support. She glanced at Witt, who was grinning like the cat who'd eaten the canary. Waving the envelope, she asked, "You know something about this, don't you?"

"Maybe you should just open it." He set his glass on

the table, then turned a chair sideways and sat, one leg crossed over the opposite knee.

"Okay, Mr. Smarty-Pants, I'll just do that." She slid her thumb beneath the flap. When she pulled out the letter, a baby blue business-size check slid from the folds. It landed face up on the table, the amount plain to see—a staggering twenty-five hundred dollars!

Heart hammering, she forced herself to draw a breath as she spread open the letter. The owners wrote that they'd recently heard from several customers about the "extraordinary and invaluable service Eventide provides for dogs that otherwise might never have received the loving care they so deserve." The letter went on to explain that the store wanted to begin with this larger onetime donation to kick off a renewal of their ongoing monthly support.

"Wow." The word whispered across her lips. "Witt, what did you do?"

"Hardly anything. One day when I was picking up some kennel supplies, I gave a handful of your new brochures to the manager and asked if he'd display them on the counter for their customers to take." He chuckled. "Apparently, the brochures were conversation starters. People you'd done portraits for and who'd been out here to see the dogs just couldn't stop talking about Eventide."

She stared again at the check and shook her head. "Did you know they were going to do this?"

"When I replenished the brochure stack last week, they sort of hinted at it." He shifted and reached for her hand. "This is all you, Maddie. It's your talent, your commitment...your heart."

A tearful laugh bubbled up, and she flicked away an

escaping droplet. "I appreciate the compliments, but you have to take credit for setting all this in motion. If you hadn't prodded me to do that first arts and crafts fair and then backed me every step of the way, I'd probably be in bankruptcy court by now. And those dogs..." Voice trailing off, she couldn't let herself imagine where her precious pups would have ended up.

"You'd never have let that happen." He scooted his chair closer so he could capture her face in his hands. "Remember, I know exactly how stubborn you are, especially when it comes to protecting your dogs."

He wasn't wrong about her stubbornness. And she hoped he was right about her resourcefulness. But as for making do without him? That was something she hoped she'd never have to find out.

The next morning, Maddie tucked the pet store donation into her purse and drove to the Elk Valley minimall. Her bank didn't have a branch in Elk Valley, but they did staff a teller window inside the grocery mart.

"Got a deposit for you, Irene." She slid the check and deposit slip across the counter.

"Oh, my." The sixtysomething teller eyed Maddie over the rims of her cat's-eye reading glasses. "Why, Maddie McNeill, I do believe this is the most money to hit the Eventide account since before..." Her expression turned sympathetic. "Since your poor grandma passed away."

"Yes, I'm hopeful the tide has turned."

"I've been hearing about your drawings—talk of the town this summer." Irene typed something into her computer terminal. "Howard's hunting spaniel was the last dog we had, but he's been gone two years now. I ought to dig out some pictures and see if you could draw him for Howard's birthday coming up. He still misses that ol' fella."

"Happy to. Just let me know."

After processing the deposit, Irene passed Maddie the receipt but kept one finger on it. "Hang on a sec, hon." Lips pursed, she studied her computer screen. "The way this account is growing, you ought to think about investing some of the money so it could earn interest. Standard savings accounts don't pay much of a return, but there are other options."

Stomach tensing, Maddie shook her head. "I prefer knowing my money is safely tucked away in my bank account."

"After what those scammers did to your grandparents, I do understand. But if you ever change your mind, we have some savvy investment counselors at the branch office in Missoula. They wouldn't steer you wrong."

With a polite thank-you, Maddie slid the receipt into her purse and reminded Irene to get in touch if she wanted a portrait of her husband's old hunting dog.

Dealing with money issues was stressful enough. She could have done without the reminder of how her grandparents had been cheated. Despite her best attempts toward a more forgiving attitude, the anger persisted.

At home later, she spent more time than usual in the play yard with the dogs. Seeing them happy and well never failed to cheer her—and to remind her why she so wanted to honor and preserve her grandparents' legacy.

Was she being *too* cautious, though? What if she really could augment the Eventide funds with a few wise and well-secured investments? Maybe tonight over supper she could persuade Witt to share his thoughts. Though he'd been hesitant about offering financial advice, she'd trust him over some random bank officer.

It was after six o'clock when Witt got home from his handyman job. By then, Maddie had already taken care of the dogs and horses and had lemon chicken in the oven. After cleaning up, he trudged to the house. Looking exhausted, he apologized for not getting home sooner to help with the animals.

"I'm perfectly capable, and anyway, you've pitched in plenty of times when I had other things going on." She handed him a tall glass of iced tea. "Sit down and take a load off while I get supper on the table."

"You're too good to me, Maddie." Before taking his seat, he massaged his low back. "I think I'm getting too old for hauling and laying paving stones."

There was a tiredness in his tone that she hadn't heard in a while. Stepping around Ranger, she found the bottle of over-the-counter pain reliever in the cupboard and set it beside Witt's tea glass. "Take a couple of these. I have an electric heating pad you can use tonight, too."

He perked up slightly as he filled his belly and the pain tablets began to kick in. After a quiet supper, she served up the last two slices of huckleberry pie with generous scoops of the vanilla ice cream she'd picked up at the market that morning.

When she set his dessert plate in front of him, he broke out in a grin. "I was hoping there was still some pie left. Ice cream, too—what a treat!"

"It's nice to feel like I can afford the occasional splurge." She savored a bite, a satisfied sigh escaping. This probably wasn't the best moment to pose her money questions, but now that she'd brought up the subject… "When I deposited that big check this morning, my friend at the teller window said I ought to consider investing some of the money that's come in this summer."

"Mmm-hmm."

She tapped her fork on the edge of her plate. "After how my grandparents lost their savings, though, the whole idea makes me nervous."

He kept his eyes lowered, as if scooping up exactly the right ratio of pie to ice cream were of the utmost importance. "You never told me about that."

"Just thinking about it makes me so angry I could spit nails." Already sorry for mentioning it, she attempted to stab an errant huckleberry. "Never mind. Let's talk about something else. Please."

Witt pushed his plate away, the last couple of bites uneaten. "Afraid I'm not much for conversation tonight. I'll help you clean up, and then if I could trouble you for that heating pad…"

Concern rising, she studied him. "Are you sure you're just tired? Not getting sick, are you?"

"I'll be fine. Like I told you, too much heavy lifting today." His smile was less than convincing. As he pushed to his feet, he winced and nearly doubled over.

She jumped up to steady him, easing him back into the chair. "That's it. You need to cancel whatever jobs you had for tomorrow and take it easy."

"Can't. The guy I partnered with to lay this patio is counting on me, and we've got at least another full workday ahead, maybe more."

"You can't work if you're hurting." She harrumphed.

"The way you're looking right now, I'm not even sure you can make it upstairs to the loft."

"I'll be fine," he repeated, but the white-knuckled fist resting on his thigh belied his assertion.

"Hand me your phone."

He twisted his head to look up at her. "What? No."

Glaring, she darted her hand out and snatched the phone from his shirt pocket, then scurried several steps away. She'd seen him call the Happy's Helpers office often enough that she knew his unlock code and how to find the number.

"Maddie—"

She turned away and tapped a few buttons. When the answering service picked up, she gave her name and said, "I'm calling for Witt Wittenbauer. He overdid it on the job today. He needs—"

"Maddie!" Two long strides closed the distance between them. He reclaimed his phone and held it to his ear. "Hello, is this Nancy? Yeah, hi, it's Witt. Everything's okay. Sorry for the mix-up."

Maddie fumed while he ended the call. "You are *not* okay. Why are you being so stubborn?"

Ranger was on his feet now. Upper lip curled, the dog moved in front of Witt.

"Easy, boy." Witt reached for the dog's collar. "She meant well." The hint of a smile returning, he whistled through his teeth. "And talk about stubborn!"

"You are so—"

His lips landed on hers in a long, gentle kiss, and whatever she'd meant to say dissipated like smoke on a breeze. He pulled her close and tucked her head beneath his chin. "Thank you for caring so much. I'm going up to the loft now and get some rest. But you have my word, if I'm still hurting this bad in the morning, I will call in sick."

She leaned away and cupped his cheek. "If you're still hurting at all—"

"Now, don't get pushy." His tone was firm, but his grin held nothing but affection. "I know my limits. I'll be careful."

"You'd better." *Because I can't lose you.* "I'll be right back with that heating pad."

Chapter Twelve

Feeding the kennel dogs with Maddie the next morning, Witt assured her a couple more OTC pain pills combined with moist heat and a good night's sleep had done the trick. He still had a few twinges but not bad enough to skip a day of work. Neglecting to wear his back brace yesterday was a mistake he wouldn't make again.

He hadn't exactly been truthful about the good night's sleep, though. After Maddie had mentioned something about her grandparents losing their savings, he'd worried all night. If they'd been victims of his former employer, could Maddie ever forgive him?

Could he ever forgive himself?

When he arrived at the job site, his partner apologized for not realizing what a big project it would turn out to be. "I've got two more guys on the way. With their muscle, we should easily finish by early afternoon."

The brawny young men, both in the Army Reserve, didn't disappoint, either in their strength or their work ethic. Shortly before two o'clock, when the homeowner signed off on the completed patio, Witt breathed a sigh of relief. With time to spare before he needed to head home, he stopped in town at Elk Valley Community of Faith. The church office was open, and the secretary showed him to Pastor Peters's study. She'd seen Witt with Ranger in church often enough that she seemed unfazed about a dog traipsing through the office.

After a handshake, the blue-jeaned pastor gestured toward a chair. "Have a seat. What can I do for you, Witt?"

Now that he was here, he didn't quite know how to broach the subject. He stalled while Ranger turned around a few times before getting comfortable on the carpet. "Well, I... I guess you know that Maddie and I are getting closer."

"Yes, and it's been good seeing you in church together this summer. I was afraid for a while that losing her grandmother had left her faith too shattered to let God work His healing."

"I know she still misses her."

"Sorcha Madigan was much loved and admired in this community. Her husband, too, before he passed away a few years back." Pastor Peters firmed his jaw. "A real shame, that was. Dennis never got over losing his savings to those scammers. It wasn't a year later when he suffered a fatal heart attack."

Fighting to keep his tone level, Witt said, "Maddie hasn't told me much about that."

"I've tried to get her to talk to me, too. Keeping to herself, bottling up her emotions..." The pastor exhaled sharply, then cast Witt a smile. "I'm thankful she has you now. You've clearly been good for her."

Witt could barely swallow. "She's been good for *me*."

Giving a nod of understanding, the pastor left the room for a moment, then returned with a glass of water and handed it to Witt. With one hip propped on the corner of the desk, he began gently, "You came by this afternoon with something specific on your mind. Ready to tell me what it is?"

He took a slow sip of water and let the coolness soothe his throat, then stared into the glass. "I've got this awful feeling my world's about to come crashing down on my head."

Softly, the pastor asked, "Any reason why?"

Gaze fixed on the toe of Pastor Peters's brown cowboy boot, Witt inhaled slowly. "It won't make sense unless I start at the beginning."

Twenty minutes later, he'd poured out everything—his earliest suspicions about what was going on within the company, how turning whistleblower had destroyed his life, and now his fear that Maddie's grandparents may have been among the many victims.

The pastor stared at him with a mixture of awe and empathy. "I knew you'd been through some hard times, but I had no idea. How much of this does Maddie know?"

"Most of it. I mean, I haven't lied, just kept some parts purposely vague. When I was going through all this stuff with the feds and lawyers and such, they convinced me it'd be safer all around if I stayed anonymous." Chest aching, he looked away. "I couldn't put my family at risk for retaliation, but the stress, the secrecy, the loss of my job and reputation…it turned out to be more than I could handle."

"That'd be an awfully heavy burden for anyone to carry." The pastor offered an understanding smile. "And now you've added Maddie to the list of people you care about."

"I was starting to feel like we—that maybe—" He

couldn't bring himself to speak aloud the words *I'm falling in love.*

"Even if Maddie's grandparents were among this company's victims, do you really think she'd hold you responsible for something you had no part in?"

"You don't get it, Pastor. I'd suspected for months that something wasn't right. Every day that I sat on that knowledge instead of reporting it meant more unsuspecting families were losing their life savings." He gave his head a brisk shake. "Spin it any way you want to, but you'll never convince me I'm free from responsibility."

Arms folded, the pastor strode to the window. "You've obviously made up your mind about your perceived guilt. So again I ask you, what did you come here for?"

The question took Witt by surprise. "I... I don't know. I guess I just wanted reassurance...and maybe a little hope."

Pastor Peters faced him with a sad smile. "There's always hope, my friend. We worship a God of hope. Hope and second chances and forgiveness beyond measure. Once you finally, *fully* believe that, what you did or didn't do in the past won't matter anymore."

"Maybe not to God, but this side of heaven, choices have consequences. And I'm living with them every single day."

With a thoughtful sigh, the pastor took his seat behind the desk. Turning to the credenza behind him, he riffled through a file drawer and removed a folder from somewhere near the back. "I don't know whether I'm about to lighten your burden or make it even heavier, but maybe I can give you at least one answer you came looking for."

Witt held his breath as Pastor Peters spread the contents of the folder across his desk. It appeared to be a collection of old newspaper clippings.

The pastor unfolded a strip of yellowed newsprint. "I saved this article from Elk Valley's weekly newspaper. The reporter did a human-interest piece on local folks, including the Madigans, who'd been defrauded by a corrupt investment company." He passed the clipping across the desk. "The article names the company and the executive officers who were charged and convicted."

Pulse hammering, Witt reached for the article. The opening paragraphs clearly identified Copper Bluff Financial Professionals along with the chief financial advisor he'd directly reported to—and who, the article said, had personally handled the Madigans' account.

He rose slowly, his hand shaking as he laid the paper on the pastor's desk. "Thank you. Not what I was hoping for, but…it is what it is."

The pastor caught his arm as he stumbled toward the door. "Stay, Witt. We can talk through this—"

"No, I… I need time to think."

As if thinking would change anything. If only he'd acted sooner, stopped second-guessing himself. If only he hadn't refused for so long to believe the evidence that had been right before his eyes!

After setting the oven timer for the shepherd's pie she'd thrown together, Maddie watched out the kitchen window hoping for a glimpse of Witt's little truck. He must have had another long workday. She prayed his back had held up and he wasn't at this very moment lying in a hospital emergency room.

It was after seven by the time he finally pulled up

beside the barn. Good thing she hadn't waited for his help with the dogs and horses. The poor man must be exhausted.

And her poor shepherd's pie was probably dry as dirt.

She finished getting supper on the table, then paced for another ten minutes waiting for him to come to the house. Should she go up and check on him? Maybe she should take a plate of food to the loft in case he was hurting too badly to come down. And if that was the case, she'd brook no arguments from him about taking tomorrow off and making an appointment to see a doctor.

Minutes later, she rapped lightly on his door. "Witt? You okay?"

It seemed forever before the door finally cracked open. "Hi. Sorry, I was…" He glanced at the foil-covered plate she held. "I'm sorry, Maddie. I should have let you know I'd be late."

"I was worried. I hope you didn't overdo it again today."

"No, no, we had extra help, and I…" His jaw muscles bunched. He looked away. "After we got done, I needed to take care of…some errands."

"That's fine." Why didn't she believe him? Forcing a smile, she thrust the plate toward him. "It's a little overcooked from sitting in the oven so long. I didn't know when to expect you."

"My fault entirely. It won't happen again." Accepting the meal, he smiled back, but there was no warmth in his expression. "Thanks, Maddie. Good night." The door whispered closed.

She remained on the landing for several long moments while she tried to understand what had just happened. Witt hadn't had one of his moody spells in so long that she'd hoped the despondency was gone for good.

And what *errands* had distracted him so thoroughly that he hadn't bothered to call or text? Had he tried to see his daughter again, or perhaps reached out to his son only to suffer yet another rejection? Though he might pretend otherwise, she sensed how badly he still missed his children.

Whatever was going on, she refused to let him shut her out. She knocked again, harder this time.

Just when she'd decided he intended to ignore her, the hinges creaked. "Did you forget something?"

"No, but you did." She planted her fists on her hips. "You apparently forgot we're friends—more than friends, I'd hoped—and that you can talk to me about anything."

"Oh, Maddie." He drew a hand down his face. "Not this time."

"What do you mean? What could be so awful that you can't tell me?"

He replied with a brisk shake of his head, then drew her into a crushing embrace that said more about his torment than words ever could.

Just as quickly, he released her, the slanting evening sun revealing his red-rimmed eyes. "You'd better go," he murmured. "And don't worry about me. I need to figure out some stuff, that's all."

"Witt—"

Again, the door closed in her face.

Angry, confused, she marched down the steps. "All right, be that way," she mumbled. If he didn't want to let her into his heart, if he wouldn't let her help carry whatever burden weighed on him, that was his loss. She certainly couldn't force him.

Returning to the house, she plopped down at the table and filled a plate for herself. One bite, though, and her appetite fled. The shepherd's pie tasted fine, if a little overcooked, but between missing Witt and her bewilderment over how he'd pushed her away, she couldn't even think about eating.

Her glance landed on Nana's embroidered table prayer. *Come, Lord Jesus...*

"Jesus," Maddie whispered, her throat closing. "I need You. Witt needs You. Help us both."

The next morning, Maddie was almost afraid to go out to the kennel to start chores. Would she find Witt there as usual, or would yesterday's unpleasantness keep him away?

Only a few days ago, they'd shared their first kiss. How could everything have gone so wrong so quickly?

Plodding across to the kennel, she glimpsed a light in the window. So he'd come down after all. Every nerve tingling, she steeled herself before entering.

Witt had just set a bowl of food in Joey's run. He straightened and smiled. "Good morning."

"Good morning." She gauged his tone and expression but detected only the same respectful courtesy he'd shown the first day they'd met. Pushing past the hurt, she asked, "How far have you gotten?"

"The bowls are filled and meds distributed. I just started delivering." He nodded on his way back to the kitchen.

She followed and picked up two of the bowls. Maybe

if she kept him talking… "Where are you working today?"

"Here and there. Small jobs, mostly." When their arms brushed as he edged past her, he flinched. "I could run late again, so don't plan on me for supper."

"Oh…okay." Her heart sank. She set a dish of puréed food in Boots's run and gave the toothless dog a scratch behind the ears. Finding her voice, she called over her shoulder, "You're coming in for breakfast this morning, though?"

"Better not. I need to get on the road soon."

She tried to convince herself he only needed a little space to process whatever was eating at him, but when his aloofness lingered over the next few days, she worried the chasm between them would soon grow too wide to bridge. When he seldom joined her for a meal anymore, there was no talking to him, no coaxing him to be honest with her. And though he was as faithful as ever with kennel and barn responsibilities, he'd taken to doing his part at times when he'd have the least amount of interaction with her.

Then Sunday morning rolled around, and when he made a weak excuse about skipping church, there was no question he was avoiding her.

No question except *why*.

When Julia came out the following Wednesday to give some checkups and immunizations, Maddie confessed her disillusionment. While she steadied Boots on Julia's portable exam table, she described the kiss in the huckleberry patch. "It was beautiful and amazing, and I was beginning to believe we had something truly special between us. Then a week ago, it was like a lead curtain dropped."

Offering a sympathetic smile, Julia moved her stethoscope around Boots's chest and abdomen. Then, removing the instrument from her ears, she faced Maddie. "I hate seeing you hurt again, but I can't say I'm surprised. I mean, consider his history—broken marriage, homelessness, a recovering alcoholic…"

"He's had some hard breaks, that's all. I've never met anyone more responsible and reliable than Witt—present company excluded," she added quickly.

Julia hiked a brow as she injected Boots with his annual vaccines. "I still think you should have done a background check. At least then you'd know what you're dealing with."

Maddie started to snap back that she knew all she needed to know about Witt—but clearly she didn't. "Even if I wanted to, I wouldn't know where to start."

"You found his children on the internet, right? So do a search using his name. In the meantime, a friend of my dad's has connections with the Montana Department of Justice. I'll see if he can dig anything up."

"Something illegal?" Maddie sputtered. "But he assured me he didn't have a criminal background."

Her friend gave her a frown that implied her utter naivete. "I'm just saying you should cover all the bases." Under her breath, she added, "Which you should have done on day one."

Swallowing a retort, Maddie returned Boots to his run. She decided it best to drop the subject for now and get on with the dogs' exams.

An hour later, Julia packed up her gear and left, but not without another not-so-subtle admonition about probing deeper into Witt's past. Maddie replied with a noncommittal wave and went to the house.

She had to admit, though—her friend did have a point. Not that she believed for a moment that Witt was untrustworthy, but how could she hope to fix things between them unless she figured out the source of the problem?

In the study, she rolled her chair up to the desk and clicked the web browser icon on her computer screen. All she had to do was type *Angus Nathaniel Wittenbauer* into the search box, but she couldn't bring herself to do it. It was one thing trying to track down his children with the hope of reuniting them. To intentionally seek out personal information about Witt himself felt like something else entirely, an invasion of privacy she could never walk back from.

No, she needed more time to think. She'd see how he acted tonight, and if she couldn't get him to open up with her, then perhaps she'd consider other measures.

But when he didn't return home until well after eight o'clock, and then didn't make an appearance the next morning until she'd already taken care of the animals, she grew desperate. Watching from the study window as his truck disappeared around the bend, she couldn't shake the sense that his withdrawal was somehow connected to losing his family. Had he begun to believe that a relationship with Maddie meant forever shutting the door on his children?

If only she could convince Witt's daughter to give him another chance. She still had Emily's number from when she'd arranged the meeting at the restaurant. It had to be worth a try.

When the young woman finally picked up the phone, her tone was icy. "I thought I made myself clear—"

"Please, don't hang up," Maddie pleaded. "If we could just talk for a moment."

Emily hesitated. "Look, Ms. McNeill, it's obvious you care about my... About Witt. But you can't possibly comprehend how badly he hurt us."

"Maybe not, but I'm trying to. And if you could only let yourself see how badly he's hurting, too, how much he regrets the pain his drinking caused—"

A harsh laugh interrupted her. "He never told you the whole story, did he?"

Maddie grew silent while everything she knew about Witt's past played across her mind on fast-forward—job loss, alcoholism, divorce, homelessness.

"Are you near your computer?" Emily asked.

Numbly, Maddie answered, "Yes."

"Then look up Copper Bluff Financial Professionals and let me know what you find."

Nausea swept through her belly. No need to do an internet search—the name was all too familiar. "What are you saying—that your father lost money to this company?"

"No. I'm saying my father was *employed* by them. He was one of Copper Bluff's investment counselors."

Doubling over, Maddie covered her mouth. It couldn't be. Witt *couldn't* have been a party to the fraud that wiped out her grandparents' life savings. Despite the court-ordered settlement, recovery of even a portion of their losses had taken years. Before she died, Nana had resigned herself to the fact that she'd likely never see the rest.

Maddie slid her thumb across the disconnect button and dropped the phone onto the desk. Had he known? Known all along who her grandparents were? Was this whole thing a setup from the start? Sure, the reclusive dog rescuer was probably as gullible as her countrified grandparents. He'd worm his way into her life, gain her trust, get her to care for him, all the while "helping" her raise funds for the sanctuary, which he'd then find a way to abscond with. Once a scammer, always a scammer.

And she'd fallen for it. Fallen hard and fast, eyes wide shut.

Well, no more. If Angus Wittenbauer thought he was pulling one over on her, his plan had backfired, because by coaxing her out of her comfort zone and encouraging her drawing talents, he'd unwittingly empowered her to get along just fine on her own.

She made up her mind. When he got home from work this evening, she'd confront him with the truth and tell him he had to leave. She would never, ever, *ever* be taken in by another man's lies.

Anger feeding her nervous energy, she needed to do something besides sit there and fume. Being with the dogs never failed to soothe her, so she marched to the kennel, intending to let the dogs out for some playtime.

But when she entered the building, the first thing she saw was Ranger in the run with Joey.

"What are you doing here, boy?" And *why*? Witt never went anywhere without his dog.

She glanced around in search of an explanation and spied a note taped to the kitchen door. Recognizing Witt's handwriting, she read the cryptic message:

> *It's time for me to move on, but I need to leave Ranger with you until I find a place that allows pets. I left an envelope with money for his food and care. I'll come for him as soon as I can. I'm sorry, Maddie. This is better for both of us.*

Ranger whined and scratched on the gate, his soft brown eyes mirroring Maddie's bewilderment. Letting the note flutter to the floor, she dug her fingers into the hair at her temples. A scammer didn't leave money to cover pet care, much less leave his beloved dog behind.

What am I missing here? Dear God, show me what's true and what isn't.

Chapter Thirteen

Witt paged through apartment listings in the booklet he'd picked up at a convenience store. Not much help so far. Either the rent was out of reach, or they didn't allow pets, or if they did, a huge deposit was required.

"Nothing yet?" Carl Anderson, his former counselor at the transitional home, sat down across the table from him. The man had been kind enough to let Witt stay over for a couple of nights in one of the empty bunks.

"There's a few I can check out." The complexes weren't in the safest part of town, and again, no pets, but to stay off the streets he'd have to take what he could get. If it meant leaving Ranger with Maddie indefinitely, he'd send more money as soon as he could.

"Wish I could let you stay longer," Carl said with a frown, "but I have to abide by regulations or our funding gets cut."

"No worries. I'll figure out something and be out of here this afternoon."

"You never said exactly why things didn't work out at the dog sanctuary. When we talked a few weeks ago, you sounded really happy."

Witt released a humorless laugh. "Can we leave it at 'things got complicated'?"

"As in…romantically?" Carl shook his head. "If this is about you feeling unworthy—"

"That part's still a work in progress. Bottom line is I don't want to risk hurting anyone else. And Maddie's been hurt enough already."

"So packing up and leaving doesn't count as hurtful?"

Guess he wasn't going to get away with sidestepping the truth. Carl knew most of it anyway. Elbows on the table, he lowered his head into his hands. "Maddie's grandparents were victims of investment fraud."

"Not the company you worked for?"

"Yep. The very same." He described what he'd learned from Pastor Peters. "How could I face her, knowing I'm partly responsible? And not just for the money her grandparents lost but the stress and worry that eventually took both their lives."

"Haven't we been over this too many times to count? You can't keep shouldering the blame for something that was outside your control. You need to accept credit for saving who knows how many people from even greater losses. In fact," Carl continued, rising to brace his hands on the table, "it's long past time you took care of a couple of overlooked items in your twelve-step program. You need to tell your ex-wife and children the truth and make amends to them."

"You know why I've never told them. My former bosses may be in prison, but they've got long reaches. If they ever found out I was the whistleblower, they could still target not just me but the people I care about."

"Witt, your kids deserve to know their father isn't one of the bad guys. And *you* deserve a relationship with them. Can't you find a way to be honest with your family while still keeping your secret?"

"I don't know… I don't know." His stomach roiled. He wished he could accept what Carl was saying, but how could dredging up the past be good for any of them? "Even if I wanted to—even if they'd listen to me after all these years—I can't disrupt their lives again. They're better off with me out of the picture."

Scoffing, Carl paced to the other side of the kitchen. "I can't force you to stop punishing yourself. I can't force you to believe you might actually be entitled to a little happiness. It's your life, Witt," he said, facing him. "You're the only one who can decide what to do with it. I only hope you have the good sense to give God a chance to weigh in on any decisions you make."

He'd been trying to, hadn't he? The Bible said to put the concerns of others first, and that was what he'd vowed to do. What did his own life matter as long as he could keep from bringing others down with him? Most of all, Maddie, who'd cracked open places in his heart that he'd thought were sealed away forever.

Quietly, he rose and tucked the apartment guide into his back pocket. "I should get going if I want to find a place before tonight."

"Hang on, Witt. Let me give you some names and numbers. There are a couple of shelters downtown—"

"Had enough of homeless shelters. I won't go that route again." He thrust out his hand. "Thank you, Carl, for everything. And I don't want you worrying about me. I fully intend to land on my feet."

"I know you will." Carl shook his hand firmly. "I'll be praying."

A few minutes later, he headed across town to see

some apartments. The affordable vacancies he looked at weren't in the best condition, but he'd survived worse. Problem was they also came unfurnished, which meant he'd need to check out some thrift stores for cheap furniture and household goods. He didn't need much to get by, but still, it was an expense he had to consider.

Next came filling out a rental application. Witt's credit had improved a bit in the past several months, but apparently not enough to satisfy a leasing agent.

"I'll have to send this to our main office for approval," the agent told him.

"How long will that take?"

"About two weeks."

Stomach sinking, Witt nodded. "I understand. You'll call me?"

"Of course. But…" The man cast him a pointed look. "You might want to keep looking, just in case."

Back in his truck, he drove around aimlessly. He could never cross the Reserve Street bridge over the Clark Fork River without recalling the frigid winters and hot summers when he'd camped out under that bridge. The city now had a secure homeless camp behind the nearby Walmart. But even if Witt's tattered tarp and sleeping bag hadn't been lost nearly three years ago the day he went into the hospital, he couldn't bear the thought of returning to street life.

Maybe he should leave Missoula, maybe try Denver or Boise or even head down to Texas. New surroundings might help him get his head on straight and his act together.

And put enough distance between him and Maddie that maybe he'd eventually be able to forget her and everything they might have had.

The thought had no sooner passed through his mind than his phone chimed with an incoming text. Best-case scenario would be the Happy's Helpers dispatcher with an emergency repair call. A little weekend overtime pay would really help right now. He pulled into the nearest parking lot to check his phone.

It wasn't Happy's Helpers. It was Maddie. Where are you, Witt? We need to talk.

Heart thudding, he stared at the message. He missed her so much, but what good would talking do? Maybe he owed her the chance to unleash her outrage on him, but what could he say in reply that would ever make things right?

For a split second he thought about blocking her number—making a clean break might be best for both of them. But then he remembered Ranger. These past few days without his dog had almost been harder than when he'd first woken up in the hospital and realized Ranger was gone.

He thought long and hard about how to answer Maddie's text. Then with a tear trickling down his cheek, he typed There's nothing more to say, except thank you for looking after Ranger. Tell him I love and miss him and will come for him as soon as I can.

His thumb hovered over the Send button. I love and miss you, too, Maddie. I'm sorry. So, so sorry.

He hit Send, then shut off his phone. It was probably too late to count on any last-minute handyman jobs anyway. Time to pick up something for tonight's supper and tomorrow's breakfast, then find somewhere to pull over in his truck for the night. Riverfront Park downtown might work, if he could find an out-of-the-way spot where he hoped any cops on patrol would leave him alone.

Surely tomorrow he'd fare better in his apartment search. Either that or he might need to consider one of the homeless shelters after all. He just needed to stay in town and keep working until he saved enough to collect Ranger and start over somewhere else.

Answer, Witt. Please answer.

Willing a reply text to appear, Maddie sat at her desk with her phone in her hand for a good ten minutes. But even though the display indicated he'd received and read her message, those longed-for three little dots signaling he was composing a response never appeared.

He'd left barely three days ago, but it felt like an eternity. It hadn't taken long for her to decide there had to be more to the story, because either she was more gullible than she ever imagined or Witt was every bit as upright and honorable as she'd sensed from the start.

She prayed with all her heart it was the latter.

Well, she couldn't stall any longer. She had less than a week to prepare for the Labor Day craft fair in downtown Missoula. And now, without Witt to cover kennel and barn chores that weekend, she didn't know what she'd do. She certainly couldn't leave the dogs unattended for the three long days she'd be hosting her pet portrait booth.

Hoping Julia might be able to help, she started to call, then at the last second realized she'd have to give an explanation for Witt's departure. She could already hear her friend's *I told you so*, which was why she'd been keeping her discovery to herself.

Unfortunately, her immediate needs didn't leave

much choice. She placed the call. "Hi, Julia. I've got a…a situation."

"Uh-oh. Is one of the dogs sick?"

"No, they're all fine. But I—I—" Her voice broke. "Witt moved out."

"Oh, no. Why? Did he get another job somewhere?"

"It's worse. It looks like you were right about him."

Julia's tone softened with compassion. "I'm so sorry, Maddie. This is one time I really, *really* didn't want to be right. Can you tell me what happened?"

Holding back tears, she described her conversation with Witt's daughter and the revelation that he'd been an investment manager with the firm that had defrauded her grandparents. "I was furious when I found out, so certain he'd been stringing me along all this time while figuring out how he could embezzle money from the sanctuary. But the day I was ready to confront him and throw him out, he'd already left." Her voice strengthening, she added, "And *he* left money for *me* so I could take care of Ranger until he finds a new place to live."

Julia's thoughtful silence lasted for several seconds. "Do you think he discovered you found out about him?"

"I don't see how he could have known." She thought back to the days before Witt had left. "He'd definitely been troubled about something, but it seemed deeply personal, not at all like he was scheming or putting on an act."

"How can you be so sure it wasn't an act? That's what con men do—as you should know all too well."

She bristled with defensiveness—for herself or for Witt, she wasn't sure. "Don't you dare compare Witt with Garrett. They are *nothing* alike."

"Is that your head talking, or your heart?"

"Can't it be both?" Sliding open the drawer where she'd tucked away that first sketch she'd made of Witt, she found herself captivated once more by those entrancing eyes. "Oh, Julia, what if I've misjudged him? Not before, but now. There has to be some misunderstanding, something we're missing. The man I've come to know could never be responsible for anything as cold and calculating as what that company did to my grandparents."

"Wow," Julia murmured. "I knew you were developing feelings for him, but…you really have fallen in love, haven't you?"

"Yeah, I think I have." Gazing at the sketch, she pressed a hand to her heart and whispered, "What am I going to do?"

"I can still ask my dad to reach out to his law enforcement friend. Knowing now what Witt was involved with, we have a place to start."

Maddie heaved a resigned sigh. "Okay, do it. I'll never be able to rest until I learn the truth, wherever it leads."

"Just…be prepared."

"That goes for you, too, in case I get to be the one who says *I told you so.*"

"Nothing would make me happier."

Remembering what had prompted her to phone Julia in the first place, she shifted the conversation to her need for help during the Labor Day fair. Julia felt certain one of the part-time vet techs from the clinic would be happy to stay at the sanctuary over the weekend to tend the dogs and horses. She promised to get back to Maddie by Monday at the latest.

Checking one item off her worry list, she turned her

attention to the Saturday-afternoon group tutoring session she'd arranged for three students needing remedial reading help. It kept her mind off Witt—temporarily, at least. But now that she'd let in the tiniest glimmer of hope, she could only pray that Witt would give her— give *them*—another chance.

Several days later, Witt awoke from a fitful sleep to the glare of a flashlight shining in his eyes and a uniformed cop rapping on his pickup window. He sat up with a start, both hands instinctively raised.

"Step out of the vehicle, please," the officer said. "Slowly."

Trying to clear his head, he eased open the door and set his feet on the pavement. "Sorry, Officer. I, uh, got sleepy and, uh…"

"Sure you haven't been drinking?" The cop swept his light across the floorboards.

"I have not, sir." At that question, his grogginess quickly dissipated. "Really, I just needed a safe place to pull over."

After another stern look at Witt, the officer seemed satisfied concerning his sobriety. "Driver's license, please."

He gingerly pulled out his wallet and handed over his license.

"Angus Nathaniel Wittenbauer, eh? That's a mouthful." The officer compared Witt's face to the license photo, then had him wait next to the patrol car while he ran the info through the system. "Everything checks out. Your place of residence says Elk Valley. So what are you doing in downtown Missoula sleeping in your truck?"

"I had to move out last week. It was kind of sudden, and I'm waiting for my new apartment to become available." It wasn't a lie, exactly. Any day now, he hoped to learn one of the three lease applications he'd submitted had been approved.

"In that case, I suggest you check into a motel. We've got a homeless problem in this area, and you wouldn't want a run-in with those bad actors."

Witt bit the inside of his cheek to keep from saying something he'd regret—whether it was revealing his current state of homelessness or accusing the officer of passing judgment on people he knew nothing about. He tucked his driver's license back into his wallet. "Yes, sir, I'll be on my way, then. Sorry to have troubled you."

Dawn was only a couple of hours away. Not much chance of finding an out-of-the-way place in time to catch a bit more shut-eye, so he drove to a convenience store. After buying himself a large coffee and a sausage biscuit, he sat in his pickup to have breakfast. He'd wrapped up a fencing repair job yesterday and hadn't gotten any work assignments yet for today, so he'd need to find something to do with the next few hours that wouldn't draw the wrong kind of attention.

He decided to hang out at the library for a while and start researching job listings and apartments in other cities. Might as well keep his options open. After lunch, he went by one of the leasing offices again hoping a little friendly persuasion would hurry along his application. A different rep was on duty, but she acted even less interested in his plight than her predecessor.

Another trip across town took him past the park area where crews were setting up tents and signage for the Labor Day weekend arts and crafts fair. His gut clenched. *That started tomorrow already?* He should have been helping Maddie get ready. And what would she do now about the dogs and horses while she manned her booth?

At least half a dozen more texts from her, plus a couple of voice mails, remained unanswered on his phone. The messages all said pretty much the same thing—Ranger misses you. Please, can't we talk this through? Call me.

He wanted to. Oh, how he wanted to!

With nothing better to do, he pulled into a parking area to watch for a bit. Then he glimpsed Maddie's Suburban across the way. He sat up straighter, his mouth dry as he scanned the area looking for her. Her red-gold halo of curls caught his eye as she spoke with someone holding a clipboard. She was probably here making sure everything was in order for her booth.

A moment later, she happened to look his way, and her brows shot up. She must have recognized his pickup. Heart thudding, he watched her say something to the clipboard lady before she turned and marched in his direction.

Go, get out of here! his brain shouted, but his frozen limbs refused to cooperate.

At the last second, he managed to start the engine. He threw the truck into gear and sped away. Several blocks later, he slowed. No sense adding a speeding ticket to his mounting problems.

Pulling into a supermarket parking lot, he pounded the steering wheel. *Coward!*

What was he afraid of, anyway? That even if he could get past her anger long enough to give his side of the story, even if he told her he'd kept his past a secret because he only wanted to protect her...

Even if he told her, *I'm in love with you, Maddie, and the thought of living the rest of my life without you is the worst torture imaginable...*

Even if he told her all that, what if she still rejected him?

Standing in the parking space Witt had just vacated, Maddie stared after him in disbelief. He'd been right here. Watching her. Knowing she'd seen him.

And he'd fled.

Coward!

She was tempted to call or text him again, but what was the use? He must have changed some setting on his phone so now she couldn't even tell if he'd received her messages, much less read them. Besides, what she needed to tell him was better said in person. *I know what you did, Witt, and I know why you did it. And I love you—for more reasons than I can count.*

Because he was anything but a coward, at least when it came to protecting the people he loved. Two days ago, Julia's father had heard back from his law enforcement friend. Through confidential sources, he'd uncovered Witt's role in bringing down Copper Bluff Financial Professionals and making sure the criminally corrupt owners and managers served long prison sentences. But because of their connections with organized crime, Witt had testified anonymously.

What kind of courage had it taken to accept public humiliation—to destroy any chance of ever again being employed in his chosen field—all for the safety of his wife and children?

At least she knew he was still in town. She'd been worried for days that he was already hundreds of miles away and she'd never see him again. For a fleeting moment, she considered inventing an urgent repair problem so she could call Happy's Helpers and request Witt. Except once he realized who wanted to hire him, he'd make some excuse to decline.

"Ms. McNeill?" The fair organizer signaled her with a wave. "I need to cover a couple more things with you before you go."

Pasting on a smile, she strode across the lawn. "Sure, what is it?"

By this time Monday, she'd almost be done with the Labor Day fair. Afterward, she could focus all her energies on finding Witt. Because—thanks to him—she wasn't such a coward anymore, herself, and when she did find him again, she had no intention of letting him get away.

Chapter Fourteen

Earlier that summer, when Maddie's tutoring students learned she'd been doing pet portraits at local fairs and special events, a few of them had excitedly volunteered to be her assistants. The middle schoolers proved far more adept at recording sales and taking payments than she'd ever be, and since Julia couldn't always take a weekend off from the veterinary clinic to help, the kids had been an answered prayer.

She understood even better now why Witt had always preferred to stay at the sanctuary with the dogs rather than man the booth with her, where the likelihood of being recognized was too great. Even though Copper Bluff Financial had been based in Butte, many clients from the Missoula area, like Maddie's grandparents, had been lured by deceptive promises of impeccable personalized service and massive returns.

As the fair drew to a close Monday evening, Maddie massaged her cramping fingers. She'd lost count of how many dog, cat, bird and rabbit portraits she'd drawn over the past three days—plus an iguana and a quite unnerving tarantula—not to mention several orders she had yet to fulfill for customers who hadn't brought their pets but would be sending her photos to work from.

"How'd we do?" she asked Stephie, her student assistant for the day.

"Totaling it up right now. You had just over five hundred dollars in sales today, so for the entire weekend it comes to…thirteen hundred forty dollars, *not* counting deposits on the special orders."

"That's unbelievable!" Happy and exhausted, Maddie whooshed out a breath. "You're a lifesaver, Steph. I'm sure glad I had you here to handle the math."

The purple-haired girl grinned. "I may be lousy at conjugating verbs, but when it comes to numbers, I got ya covered."

No way would she correct the girl's grammar at a moment like this. "Let's get packed up. I'm ready to go home."

Carrying her supplies to the Suburban, she kept an eye out for Witt. All weekend long, she'd caught glimpses of a slim, blue-jeaned figure slipping through the milling crowd, or thought she recognized a baseball cap tipped at a certain angle. She'd been unable to shake the feeling that even if she hadn't spotted him, he was always somewhere nearby watching over her.

There *had* to be a way to find him, to get him to listen to her, to convince him she needed him. To tell him she'd fallen into the deepest forever kind of love and desperately wanted him to come home.

It took most of the following week to recover from the long weekend and catch up on things at the sanctuary. An additional benefit from doing all these fairs was growing interest from animal lovers offering to volunteer a few hours a week or month to help with kennel chores and love on the dogs. Maddie hadn't taken time yet to formulate a plan for accepting volunteers, but as busy as her pet portraits and tutoring schedule kept her, she probably shouldn't put it off much longer.

After church the following Sunday, Pastor Peters pulled her aside. "Any word from Witt?"

Earlier that week, in need of guidance, she'd shared what she'd been told about Witt's past, only to learn Witt had confided in the pastor before he'd moved out. Learning Witt had seen the newspaper article about her grandparents explained so much about his withdrawal in the days before he left.

"No word at all," she said, her throat tightening. "And Ranger's getting more and more depressed every day that Witt's gone."

"Just Ranger, eh?" The pastor smiled knowingly.

"No, not just Ranger. I'm sick with missing him, Pastor. If only I knew where to look."

"Have you tried the transitional home where he was living before?"

"I spoke with Carl Anderson a few days ago. He said Witt did stay there for a couple of days, but he hasn't heard from him since. All he knows is that Witt was hoping to find an affordable apartment."

"So he must still be working for the handyman service. Have you tried calling his employer?"

"That was a dead end. They won't give out personal information."

"Figures. But at least we can assume he's staying somewhere in the area."

"Yes, but for how long?" Maddie flicked a drop of moisture from beneath her eye. "What if he leaves town? How will I ever find him then?"

The pastor scratched his chin. "It occurs to me that there's someone else as invested in finding Witt as you are. Maybe you should enlist his aid."

For a moment, she couldn't imagine whom Pastor Peters could be talking about. Then it hit her. "Ranger." Her heart lifted. "Do you really think he could track Witt down?"

"I think it can't hurt to try."

Buoyed with renewed hope, Maddie rushed home. She'd drive Ranger up and down every street in Missoula if she had to. And why not start this afternoon?

Within the hour, she'd changed from church clothes into jeans, T-shirt and sneakers. She was almost too excited to have lunch but made herself eat half a ham sandwich. She packed a cooler with snacks for herself, treats for Ranger and bottled water for them both. When she went to fetch him from the kennel, Joey made it known he wouldn't be left behind, and since two noses were better than one, she loaded both dogs into the Suburban. With Joey in the back seat and Ranger riding shotgun, she said a quick prayer and set off.

Exiting I-90 at Wye, she followed Broadway past the airport. Before she turned south on Reserve, she lowered the windows enough to let the dogs poke their noses out. "Find Witt," she said. "Come on, Ranger, you can do it."

The dog seemed to understand. Sitting up on full alert, he swept his head in all directions. Maddie thought she noticed a slight reaction as they crossed the Reserve Street bridge, once a popular camping spot for the city's homeless population. Recalling Missoula now had an authorized homeless encampment behind Walmart—and praying with all her heart that Witt *wouldn't* have found himself in such dire conditions again—she turned off the main road and circled back through the area. Ranger sniffed a few times but then lost interest.

"Okay, where to next, fellas?" Best case for Witt was that he'd moved into an apartment by now, but on his income, he'd have looked for something in a less expensive part of town.

Spotting a convenience store, she darted inside and grabbed one of the free apartment guides. Back in the car, she checked addresses for a few of the lower-priced complexes and then got back on the road.

Three hours later, she had nothing to show for her efforts except an empty cooler and two tired dogs. Discouraged, she turned toward home. Reaching across to stroke Ranger's head, she said, "We'll try again tomorrow, boy. I'm not giving up."

Just before dawn on Wednesday, Witt's phone alarm woke him from a fitful sleep. He sat up carefully, his back stiff from too many nights sleeping on his friend Justin's couch. Justin also worked for Happy's Helpers, and when Witt mentioned he was having trouble getting approved for an apartment lease, Justin said he was welcome to stay at his place until something else worked out.

Today he had another job at David and Alicia Caldwell's house, this time for some interior painting. The fact that they'd called and asked for him seemed like an answered prayer. He recalled their son was a building contractor in Texas, and if he was hiring, his parents' recommendation of Witt could make starting over somewhere else a little easier.

By eight o'clock, he was tapping on the Caldwells'

back door. David greeted him with a warm smile and a steaming mug of fresh coffee. "Great to see you again, Witt. How have you been?"

Accepting the coffee, he gave an evasive shrug. "Life's had its ups and downs lately."

Alicia appeared at her husband's side with a plate of breakfast pastries. "Good morning. Here, have a couple of these before you get started."

"Thanks, that's mighty kind." And a lot more enjoyable than the stale bran flakes he'd had at Justin's.

The Caldwells invited him to have a seat at the patio table. Handing him a napkin, Alicia said, "I hear Maddie's been making quite a splash at arts and crafts fairs around town."

"She's done real well. I know she appreciates you giving her that first opportunity."

"It took your persuasive powers to convince her, though." Smiling, Alicia arched a brow. "You two seemed pretty close last time I saw you. Any developments on that front?"

The bite of cheese Danish in Witt's mouth lost all flavor. Attempting to swallow, he set the remainder on his napkin.

"I didn't mean to pry," Alicia said softly. "Are you okay?"

He nodded. "It's…complicated. I moved to town a couple of weeks ago, and I, uh…" Maybe this was the time to say something about getting in touch with their son. Without going into unnecessary detail, he mentioned he'd been thinking about leaving Montana and getting a fresh start somewhere, possibly in Texas.

The Caldwells looked both disappointed and concerned, but said they'd be happy to put in a good word

for him with their son. He thanked them, then hurried
to finish his coffee and pastry so he could get to work
and avoid more questions.

Later, as he masked the woodwork in the guest room
he'd be painting, a commotion outside reached his ears.
It sounded like the frantic barking of dogs—at least two,
maybe more. The Caldwells didn't have a dog. Neighbors, maybe? One of them sounded a lot like Ranger,
but that was impossible. He couldn't tell if the dogs
were fighting or excited, but something sure had them
riled up.

"Witt," David called up the stairs. "You'd better get
down here, fast!"

Must be some kind of trouble. He hoped nobody was
hurt. Reaching the front hallway, he could hear the dogs
louder than ever. He skidded to a stop behind David,
who stood facing out the open front door. "What's going
on?"

David moved to one side, and a second later, Witt
found himself flat on his back. Eighty pounds of furry
canine pinned him down, while a familiar wet tongue
slathered his face with dog slobber.

"Ranger, take it easy!" Stunned into laughter, he
grabbed the dog's cheek fur. "You silly ol' dog. What
are you doing here? And how—"

Before he could finish the question, Joey joined in,
yipping and prancing like a puppy. With both dogs in
his face now, Witt struggled to sit up. When he did, he
glimpsed a woman's silhouette framed in the doorway.
Backlit by morning sun, her features were a dark blur,
but the halo of strawberry-blond hair left no doubt it
was Maddie.

Arms akimbo, she stepped closer. "Angus Nathaniel

Wittenbauer. Do you have any idea what you've put me through these past three weeks? I am so mad at you, I could scream."

Scrambling out from under the dogs, he pushed to his feet. "Maddie, I'm sorry."

"You should be!" Her voice shook, rising on every word. "I thought we trusted each other, but I couldn't have been more wrong. How could you, Witt? How could you let me down like this?"

"I—I know. I'm so, so sorry," he repeated. With the dogs continuing their antics all around his legs, he could barely keep his balance, much less form a coherent thought. He tugged on Ranger's collar. "Sit, boy. Calm down, okay?"

David intervened, handing Joey's dangling leash to Maddie. "Why don't you two take the dogs out to the backyard. You can sit on the deck and talk this out."

As the Caldwells ushered them down the hall and out to the deck, Witt felt like he was being carried along on a raging river. He was supposed to be working for the Caldwells, not inflicting his personal problems on them. And Maddie—what was she even doing here? How had she known where to find him? The Happy's Helpers dispatcher would never have given out his location.

Next thing he knew, he was back in his chair at the patio table with Maddie seated near him. The plate of pastries reappeared, along with a carafe and two coffee mugs. Alicia patted Witt on the shoulder before slipping inside and quietly closing the door.

Apparently satisfied at finding Witt, the dogs had settled down some. They seemed more interested now in sniffing all the strange new smells in the Caldwells' backyard.

He drew a bolstering breath. "Maddie, I—"

"No," she interrupted, hand upraised. "I get to speak first."

Stomach quivering, he clamped his lips together and nodded.

She gripped the armrests as if gathering strength from somewhere deep inside. Her gaze faltered for several seconds before landing squarely on him. Those riveting turquoise eyes bored through him like ice shards. "You left," she said flatly. "You left without giving me the courtesy of a face-to-face goodbye."

He lowered his head. "I didn't know how—"

"I'm not finished. Look at me."

Swallowing, he fought for the courage to raise his eyes.

"What really hurts," she went on, her tone hardening even more, "is that you didn't tell me the truth—the whole truth—from the very beginning."

"I can't say enough how sorry I am. If I'd had any idea—" His throat closed. How much did she already know? "Pastor Peters told me what happened to your grandparents. I was working for the investment company—"

She waved a hand. "Yes, I know all about it. I know everything, Witt."

No wonder she was so angry—angry enough to track him down and confront him for his role in obliterating the Madigans' life savings. "I should have told you. But I couldn't...couldn't bear seeing the revulsion in your eyes when you found out."

"Revulsion?" Her stare turned to bewilderment. "Witt, I know you were the whistleblower, and I know you had to keep silent to protect your family." Her chin

quivered. "What I'm so upset about is that you didn't trust me…trust *us*."

Us? "I—I didn't think—"

"That's the truest thing you've said today. You *didn't think*." She swung toward him and clasped his hands. Tears filled her eyes. "Oh, Witt! When did you decide I don't get a say in our future?"

He blinked at the wetness slipping down his own face. "I thought I'd lost any chance of a future with you."

"You silly man." Smiling tenderly, she grazed his cheek with her thumb. "Don't you know I'm in love with you?"

"But I don't deserve—"

"Don't say another word." She rose and stood before him. Cradling his face in her hands, she bent and pressed her lips to his.

When the kiss ended, he couldn't have formed a rational sentence if he'd tried. Unless this was all part of a waking dream, he'd heard her say it plain as day— *I'm in love with you.*

His chest ached so badly that he could hardly draw a breath. Gently taking her wrists, he eased her back a step so he could stand. "Maddie, I… I need some time."

Confusion and disappointment stole the glow from her eyes. "What do you mean?"

Turning to brace his hands on the deck rail, he watched the dogs roaming the yard, blissfully ignorant of his turmoil. "For most of the past eight years," he began with a sigh, "I've shouldered an almost unbearable burden—guilt for what happened to all those trusting people, and then shame for how I destroyed everything I cared about. Preachers, counselors, friends—

they've all done their best to convince me I could let it all go, and believe me, I've tried."

He shifted to face Maddie, and his heart clenched. "Then I met you, and for the first time since my life went topsy-turvy, I actually *wanted* to lay down the guilt and shame. I wanted to be the kind of man who'd be worthy of hearing a woman as beautiful and kind and caring as you say those words, *I love you.*"

"But you are, Witt. You have to believe—"

Laying two fingers against her lips, he offered a sad smile. "I hear you, Maddie, but this is between me and God now, and we've got to do some serious talking—or rather, I've got to do some serious listening. So please, just give me a bit more time."

A thoughtful frown etched a crease between her brows. "All right, on one condition. You have to move home to the loft. Tonight."

He was about to tell her it wasn't such a good idea, and then Ranger bounded up the steps and pawed at his legs. Guess his dog wasn't willing for them to spend one more day apart. "All right," he agreed. "I'll be… I'll be *home* tonight."

"In time for supper." She narrowed one eye.

"Yes, ma'am. In time for supper."

Maddie's insides were shaking as she loaded Joey into the back seat of the Suburban. She couldn't have lured Ranger to come home with them if she'd offered him a twenty-ounce T-bone smothered in bacon. Leaving the dog behind could turn out to be a huge mistake, though, because now Witt wouldn't have any reason to return to the sanctuary.

Except possibly one, and she could only pray she

wasn't wrong about his feelings for her. His eyes—those eloquent brown eyes that had captivated her from day one—revealed more than words could ever say. And the message she'd read there moments ago spelled out a love as deep as her own.

Alicia Caldwell had walked out to the driveway with her. "The dogs really found Witt by picking up his scent? That's incredible."

"After driving up and down just about every street in Missoula the past few days, I was losing hope." Maddie gave Joey a pat before closing the car door. "Then when we turned at the entrance to your neighborhood, Ranger immediately perked up. And the rest," she finished with a weak laugh, "is history."

"I have a feeling your story is only just beginning." The slender woman drew her into a hug. "Whatever is going on with you two, trust God to work it out."

"Thank you. I'm trying." Maddie opened the driver's-side door. "Oh, and thank you again for your generous donations to Eventide. I should have come by much sooner to express my gratitude in person."

"No, I think today was actually the perfect day for your visit." Alicia lowered her voice. "Witt may not admit it yet, but he needed you to find him…before he made a decision I'm sure he'd come to regret."

Maddie tilted her head. "What do you mean?"

Alicia confided Witt's mention of possibly moving to Texas and going to work for her son. "I've only heard part of Witt's story, and even that much would be enough to devastate a weaker man." Sadness clouded her expression. "My son lost his family, too, and finding himself—finding God again—was a long, hard road."

"I'm so sorry," Maddie whispered.

"And then he met someone." Alicia's face brightened. "He fell in love all over again and is happier now than I have ever known him to be."

Looking toward the house, Maddie bit the inside of her lip. "So there's hope for Witt and me?"

"Life has taught me that when we let go of our own will and allow the Lord to direct our steps, there is always hope." Alicia smiled over her shoulder, where her husband was puttering around in the garage, then added softly, "And far greater good than we could think to ask for or imagine."

Maddie suspected there was more to the Caldwells' story, too, yet the deep and abiding love they shared was undeniable. More every day, she longed for such a love with Witt, a love strong enough to endure every trial and overcome any obstacle.

Driving toward Elk Valley, she pondered Alicia's words about hope and faith. She'd always thought Witt had the stronger faith and that he'd been the one to lead her back to God. But maybe all along they'd needed each other to spackle the cracks, to shore up the places where their personal bulwarks of faith had weakened.

The thought reminded her of the passage from Nehemiah that Pastor Peters had preached on last Sunday—the Jewish remnant working side by side to rebuild Jerusalem's wall. The work was hard and dangerous, but despite attacks from without and temptations from within, they persevered.

With the Lord's help, you and I will persevere, too, Witt. I know we will.

At home, she wasn't sure what to do with herself until evening. Not that she didn't have plenty on her task list—an after-school tutoring session, a few more pet portraits to complete and of course the animals to tend to. But her heart, her mind, her entire being would be striving toward the moment she glimpsed Witt's battered white pickup lumbering up the lane.

Chapter Fifteen

Painting was soothing work. Dip the roller in the tray, load it with paint, then spread the new color across the wall in long, smooth strokes. With each repetition, the old, faded hue methodically disappeared, along with every nick, scratch and smudge. At the end of the day, with the masking tape removed, drop cloths folded and furniture moved back into place, it was a fresh, new room.

A fresh, new life.

"Behold, I make all things new."

Why must he struggle daily to trust that God in His great mercy truly could paint over the ugliness of a messed-up life?

David stepped back from the chest of drawers they'd repositioned between the windows. "This looks great."

Nodding, Witt surveyed the finished guest room. "You'll be ready for company in no time."

"Alicia's invited our Texas family to come up for Thanksgiving." David chuckled. "If they all show up, we'll have a houseful and then some."

The innocent remark scraped an old wound in Witt's

heart. His last Thanksgiving with family was a day he'd tried to forget. It was pretty much a blur anyway, considering he'd been on his second case of beer by the time dinner was served. The next few years his turkey and dressing had been dished up by volunteers at soup kitchens or church halls.

Then he thought of Maddie and all the pleasant meals and conversations he'd enjoyed at her table. Hope rose in his chest. She loved him. He loved her. He didn't need anyone else.

Except God. He'd always need the Lord. *Help me, Father. Help me accept Your forgiveness for all the ways I've failed, and help me forgive myself.*

Alicia looked in from the hallway. "Lovely! This shade of green will go perfectly with the new bedspread I ordered."

Ranger had made himself a nest in the folded drop cloths Witt had stacked by the door. He nudged the dog to his feet and gathered up the cloths. "I'll be back first thing in the morning to start on the next room."

"Don't rush over." Alicia cast him a knowing look. "Have a nice, leisurely breakfast with Maddie." She hooked her arm through his and ushered him toward the stairs. "In fact, you should be on your way right now. She'll be waiting for you."

That bubble of hope expanded. The running battle he'd held with himself all day was about to be lost—or won, depending on one's point of view. He was ready to wave the white flag—to surrender his guilt, his shame, his unworthiness, his fears.

He was ready to go home to the woman he loved.

Except he couldn't show up empty-handed, not if he wanted to court her like a real gentleman—and Maddie

McNeill deserved to be courted, to be treated like the beautiful, gifted, caring woman she was.

At the bottom of the stairs, he halted. "Any suggestions where I could pick up a dozen roses? And maybe some chocolates?"

Alicia looked at her husband and laughed.

"I know just the place," David said. Winking, he lowered his voice to a stage whisper. "I do have a bit of experience in the fine art of kissing and making up."

Wearing a coy grin, Alicia patted David's cheek. "Practice makes perfect."

Armed with directions to the Caldwells' favorite florist and gift shop, Witt set off. It felt right having Ranger at his side again. Chuckling, he reached over to scratch the old boy's neck. "You're the best wingman ever. And don't you worry. I will never leave you behind again."

An hour and a half later, he aimed his little truck up the lane to Eventide Dog Sanctuary. Everything looked quiet at the house and kennel. It was late enough that Maddie would have already fed the dogs and horses and settled them in for the evening. Leaving the flowers and candy in the truck in case Maddie happened to be looking out her kitchen window, he hurried upstairs to the loft. No way he'd step inside her kitchen without cleaning up and changing out of his work clothes. Wouldn't hurt to shave off his five-o'clock shadow while he was at it.

Dressed in clean jeans and his Sunday-best button-down shirt, he ran a comb through his damp hair. It was getting a little thin on top and a little grayer at the temples, but not too bad for a guy his age. Most days, especially after a long day on the job, he felt every bit of his nearly fifty-two years and then some. But tonight he felt seventeen again, about to ask his best girl to the prom.

He glanced at Ranger, who'd been tracing a path between Witt and the door. "Oops, you haven't had your supper either. We'll remedy that right quick when we get downstairs. But first…" He rummaged through a bureau drawer and found a clean red bandanna. "Let's try this on for size."

Ranger sat proudly as Witt knelt to tie the kerchief around his neck.

"There you go," he said, standing. "Now we're both dressed for the occasion."

Downstairs, he detoured to the kennel to feed Ranger. Once the dog finished, they returned outside and retrieved the roses and chocolates from the pickup. No way to conceal what he carried as he strode to Maddie's back door, so he squared his shoulders and started across the yard.

Oh, Lord, my ever-present help, give me strength!

Savory aromas filled the kitchen as Maddie peeked into the slow cooker to check the pot roast one more time. The carrots and onions looked done, and the juices were thickening nicely. She only needed to heat the bacon-seasoned green beans and mash the potatoes.

It felt wonderful to have someone to cook for again besides herself—but that was far from the only reason she'd missed Witt. Recalling how she'd kissed him earlier, she pressed one hand to her fluttering heart. When she'd left the Caldwells' this morning, she hadn't been entirely confident she could count on Witt's promise to be home for supper. Seeing him drive up half an hour ago, she'd been beyond relieved.

Returning to the stove, she glanced out the kitchen window as Witt crossed the yard—with roses in his arms! And was that a box of chocolates, too?

She patted the loose bun she'd coiled at her crown, thankful she'd taken extra time with her appearance this evening. Nothing fancy, but she'd chosen a plaid flannel kimono cardigan over a white turtleneck and her nicest pair of jeans. And though she didn't often wear jewelry, a pair of thin gold hoops dangled from her earlobes.

Witt's tap on the outer door made her jump. Apparently, his time away made him feel like he couldn't just let himself into the mudroom as he used to. Barely controlling the tremor in her voice, she called, "It's open. Come on in!"

Hearing the click, she whirled around and pretended to give all her attention to stirring the beans. It wouldn't do to appear too anxious.

Behind her, Witt roughly cleared his throat. "'Evening, Maddie. Something smells mighty good."

"Thank you. I hope you like pot roast." She screwed her eyes shut. She'd served him pot roast any number of times since he'd come to live at the sanctuary, and he'd loved it every time. "I mean, um, it's a little different recipe and—"

"Maddie." His voice was softly commanding.

She laid aside her wooden spoon and slowly turned. At the close-up view of those gorgeous red roses, each one a perfect bloom, she couldn't stifle a gasp. "Oh, my."

With a slight bow, he laid the bouquet in her arms, then handed her the sparkly heart-shaped box. "This is my utterly inadequate way of apologizing for…for everything. Maddie, if you'll allow me, I want to do things right this time. I want to try again to be the man you deserve."

If she weren't holding all of his lovely gifts, she'd wrap him in a hug and never let go. Then a clatter on the stove reminded her she'd better not let the vegetables burn. Sniffing back a tear, she nodded toward a cupboard. "If you wouldn't mind getting a vase for these flowers, I'll finish getting dinner on the table."

When she was ready to serve the meal, she saw that Witt had placed the roses in the center of the table. He pulled out her chair for her, then took his own seat. As always, Ranger plopped on the floor between them, a contented look on his furry face. It was good to see the old dog happy again.

It was good to feel happy again, herself.

They didn't talk much during dinner, which was okay with Maddie. She was doing well to eat and swallow over the euphoric ache in her chest. Instead of the mint chocolate chip ice cream she'd planned for dessert, she opened the box of chocolates, and they savored two apiece.

When the dishes were done and the leftovers put away, Witt invited her to take a walk with him. There was a nip in the September evening air, so she wrapped herself in a heavier shawl and tucked her arm beneath Witt's as they started down the lane, Ranger ambling alongside. Cool autumn nights had begun to paint the cottonwood leaves a burnished gold, and as the sun slipped behind the mountains, the last rays set the treetops a-shimmer. With her head resting against Witt's shoulder, Maddie sighed and wished these moments could last forever.

They'd reached the end of the lane. As they watched

the last remnants of sunlight fade, he kissed her temple. "What are you thinking?"

"I'm thinking how glad I am that you're home again. And how very much I love you." She shifted to look up at him, her gaze pleading. "I'm also thinking how much I long to hear those words from you."

He looked momentarily taken aback before giving an embarrassed chuckle. "I've said the words a thousand times in my head but never found the courage to say them out loud. I do love you, Maddie McNeill. I love you a thousand times more than those three little words can ever express."

Then, encircling her in his arms, he kissed her.

Stars filled the black expanse of sky. With not even a sliver of moon overhead, Witt used the flashlight on his cell phone to illumine their path back to the house.

Beneath the porch light, he kissed her once more. "I'm going to say good-night. But before I do, I want you to save Saturday evening for me, because I want to take you on a real date. How does dinner and a movie sound?"

Heart thrilling, she blinked in surprise. "It sounds absolutely lovely." Then she added quickly, "But until then, meals together as usual, right?"

"And morning and evening chores, as well." His smile turned wistful. "Those are the happiest moments of my day."

She sighed. "Mine, too."

"Then good night," he said, backing away. "I'll see you in the morning."

Gazing after Witt and Ranger as they strode toward the barn, Maddie felt awash with happiness. Witt may have courtship in mind, but she hoped it would be a short one, because she longed for the day when a kiss good-night wouldn't mean watching him walk away.

Dating again—at his age? He'd been courting Maddie—yes, he preferred the old-fashioned term over *dating*—for about a month now, and he'd never been happier.

He and Linda had been happy once, too, their early years blessed with love and many pleasant memories. Even though he hadn't always been the best husband and father, he'd cherished watching his precious babies grow into toddlers, start grade school, make friends, learn music and sports.

Some days it felt like only yesterday. Others, like a whole other lifetime. Which it was, really. He wasn't merely older, he was *different*. Everything he'd experienced over the past decade had changed him in ways he was still figuring out. He had regrets, and plenty of them. But—praise God!—he also had hope.

On a brisk October Saturday, Maddie suggested they take the horses out for a ride. Snow capped the distant mountains, but the sun was warm and the sky overhead boasted a brilliant blue, a perfect day for taking in the radiant fall colors adorning the foothills.

Beside a rippling stream, they dismounted to rest a bit. While the horses munched on tufts of grass, Witt and Maddie sat on a fallen log nearby and enjoyed a snack of granola bars and bottled water. Joey hadn't been up to a lengthy trek, but Ranger had come along. Witt fed him a few of the dog treats he'd brought, then poured water for him into a collapsible bowl.

When Maddie casually glanced at her phone for the

third or fourth time in the past half hour, Witt fought a wave of apprehension. "Expecting a call?"

"No, just checking the time." Her innocent smile definitely seemed to be hiding something.

He looked at her askance. "What do you have up your sleeve, Maddie McNeill?"

Looping her arm through his, she patted his hand. "Don't be angry—promise me."

"I could never be angry with you, honey." An uneasy laugh escaped. "But now you've got me a little worried."

"Well, you did agree that I could plan our date tonight. So…" She smiled sweetly, those amazing bluegreen eyes boring a hole through his heart. "I arranged something special."

His brow furrowed. "Why would I be mad about that?"

"You'll find out soon enough." She stood abruptly and went to gather up Sunny's reins. "We should head back."

Shaking off his doubts, he climbed on Sage. Maddie was already several yards ahead, so he nudged his horse into a trot to catch up. Maddie kept the pace just fast enough so he couldn't pepper her with more questions. Guess he'd have to wait and see what surprises she had in store.

It was nearing four o'clock when they reached the barn. With the horses returned to their stalls, Maddie seemed in a hurry to get the kennel dogs cared for. As soon as they finished, she started for the house. "I'll drive us tonight," she said over her shoulder. "Be ready at five thirty, okay?"

"Okay, but it'd sure help to have some idea where we're going."

"It won't be fancy. I'll be wearing my nice jeans again." Her quick smile gave nothing away. "See you in a bit!"

Exhaling sharply, he looked down at Ranger. "I don't know about this, fella." Witt had mostly gotten over last summer's ugly encounter with Emily. As happy as he'd been this past month, he didn't think he could handle more surprises like that one.

At five fifteen, he brought Ranger down to the kennel and settled him in with Joey for the evening. "Much as I'd prefer to have you along for moral support, I have no idea what to expect."

When he exited the kennel, Maddie was on her way out to the carport. His breath hitched. One look at her in those slim indigo jeans and hip-length purple sweater, and he was a goner. Whatever she'd arranged for tonight, as long as she was by his side, he'd be just fine.

"You look nice," he said, greeting her with a kiss.

"You, too." Leaning close, she straightened the lapels of his jacket. "Ready to go?"

He grimaced. "As vague as you've been, I'm not real sure."

She tenderly touched his cheek. "You trust me, right?"

"You know I do."

"Then get in the car and don't ask any more questions."

He had to bite his tongue a few times, but he managed to keep silent as Maddie headed toward town. He'd assumed they were going into Missoula for dinner at some special place, but when she turned the opposite direction and drove straight to Elk Valley Community of Faith, he couldn't have been more confused.

"We're going to *church*?"

Her hand shook slightly as she put the gearshift in Park. "Trust me a little bit longer, Witt. Please."

He took note of a few other vehicles in the lot, including the pastor's maroon truck. "Wait—this isn't some kind of shotgun wedding thing, is it? Because I have every intention—"

"No, nothing like that!" The look she cast him was somewhere between disbelief and compassion. With a rough sigh, she said, "Just come inside with me. It'll be okay, I promise."

If she'd sounded a little more confident, he might feel a little better about the whole thing.

When he stepped around the Suburban, she seized his hand as if to be sure he wouldn't escape, then led him around to the side entrance and down the corridor to the pastor's office.

Had she decided they needed counseling? Probably not a bad idea, but...

"Welcome." Pastor Peters met them in his doorway. With a glance over his shoulder, he said, "Good, we're all here now."

We? Who else was here? And *why?*

Maddie nudged him forward. "Go on in, Witt. It's okay."

The pastor stepped aside, and Witt eased past him. When he glimpsed the three people seated across the room, all looking uneasily at him, he froze.

Then Linda—*Linda?*—stood and strode toward him. Tears in her eyes, she took his face in her hands. "Oh, Witt, you silly, stubborn and incredibly courageous man. If only you'd told us. If only we'd known."

"Daddy." Emily came up beside her mother and

reached for his hand. "I—I'm so sorry for how I treated you that day."

Speechless, Witt could only stare in disbelief.

Then a brown-haired young man approached. "Hey, Dad."

"Trent?" Witt's voice broke. He could barely see through his own tears. He swept all three of them into his arms and sobbed uncontrollably.

Time seemed to stop as he hugged his family—the family he'd thought he'd lost forever. As a semblance of control returned, Pastor Peters handed him a wad of tissues and gently moved him toward the sitting area. Mopping his eyes, he sank onto one end of a small sofa. Linda and Trent took the chairs across from him, but Emily, perched on the sofa arm, hadn't let go of his hand.

He glanced across the room, where Maddie stood near the pastor. "How?" He stretched his free hand toward her. "How'd you make this happen?"

Swiping at her cheeks, she came and sat beside him. "I realized that until you made things right with your family, there'd always be a part of you that would never heal. Linda and your children needed to hear the truth about what you did and why, so I asked Pastor Peters to help me reach out to them."

"And we can't thank you enough," Linda said, wiping her eyes. "All the lost years, all you went through alone—I'm so, so sorry, Witt."

Love surged as he looked across at the woman he'd once been married to, then at his all-grown-up children. "To protect you, I'd do it all over again. I'm only sorry I let my weakness ruin everything we had."

Pastor Peters moved closer. "Your secret's still safe,

Witt. Enough time has passed that nobody would question your family's forgiveness or your desire to reconnect."

It sounded too good to be true. Still in shock, not only at reuniting with his family but that Maddie had arranged all this, he stood shakily. "I—I need a minute."

Taking Maddie's arm, he led her out to the corridor. "I hardly know what to say," he murmured, holding her close. "This is the kindest gift you could ever have given me. Maddie, I love you so much."

"And I love you with all my heart." Eyes shining, she used her thumb to brush away a drop of moisture on his cheek. "In the car earlier, you started to say something about your intentions. Well, Angus Wittenbauer, I have a few of my own, and though they don't involve a shotgun, they do involve a preacher."

He kissed her then, long and deep and with an abundance of happy tears. As long as he lived, he'd thank the Lord for one snowy April day and a lady with a leaky kennel roof.

Epilogue

❧

Valentine's Day, four months later

Maddie surveyed the dining room table. She could barely remember the last time she'd used the room, much less Nana's good china and table linens.

And she'd certainly never prepared a formal dinner for this many people. Besides herself and Witt, there'd be Emily and her husband, Kurt; Trent and his girlfriend; Linda and her new husband, Ed; and Pastor and Mrs. Peters. Plus Julia, of course, and Witt's friend Carl Anderson.

Hosting her own wedding *and* the reception? *What had she been thinking?*

The back door clicked, and a moment later, Witt called to her from the mudroom. "Is it safe to come in?"

"Absolutely not! The groom is not permitted to see the bride before she walks down the aisle."

A pause. "We have an aisle?"

"Figuratively speaking." They'd arranged to be married in Maddie's living room. With only their closest friends and family in attendance, they only had to move in a few extra chairs from the dining room.

"Well, how can I help you finish setting up if you won't let me in the house?"

"You'll have to wait till I go to my room to change." She adjusted the heart-shaped centerpiece. Then, glancing at the clock, she sucked in a panicked breath. "Which should have happened twenty minutes ago!"

Spinning around, she smacked into Witt's chest. He enfolded her in a soothing embrace. "Take it easy, hon. Everything's going to go just fine. And as for silly wedding traditions, we're not exactly kids anymore. Besides," he said with a chuckle, "we saw each other only a few hours ago for chores and breakfast."

She tucked her head against his shoulder. "I know. But this is my first trip down the aisle—figuratively or otherwise—and I want it to be perfect."

He kissed her forehead. "How can it not be, with God watching over us? He's sheltered us in the palm of His hand since the day we met." Giving an appreciative sniff, he added, "And what could be more perfect than getting married on Valentine's Day in a house filled with the aroma of a roast in the oven?"

"Oh, you!" She smacked his arm. "Really, I have to get dressed. People could start arriving any time now."

"No worries. I'll answer the door and make everybody comfortable. You go finish getting beautified, my radiant bride."

How could he be so calm? She started for the hallway. "Send Julia back the minute she gets here."

"Your wish is my command, milady."

Men. Honestly.

She was just slipping into her dress when Julia peeked in. "Oh, Maddie, you look amazing! Here, let me get the zipper."

"Thanks. I'm a nervous wreck today." Standing before the mirror, she smoothed her hands along the seams of the ankle-length lace-covered gown. "Are you sure this dress isn't too youthful for me? Did I go completely overboard with the whole white-dress-and-veil thing?"

"You're never too old to wear the wedding gown of your dreams. You've waited long enough for this, Maddie. Enjoy every moment."

Voices beyond the door indicated more guests had arrived. A moment later, someone knocked. "Maddie? It's Alicia Caldwell."

She nodded for Julia to invite her in, then greeted the woman with a hug. "Alicia, I'm so glad you came."

"We wouldn't have missed this special day. Also, I have a little gift for you." She opened a palm-size velveteen box to reveal a delicate necklace. The tiny gold pendant was the profile of a dog centered inside an open heart. "When I saw it, I immediately thought of you and Witt and what brought you together. I gave him a matching lapel pin."

"It's perfect. Thank you so much!" She turned and gazed into the mirror, lifting her hair so Alicia could fasten the clasp.

Julia had stepped out for a moment. Returning, she said, "Everyone's here. The harpist said to give her a nod whenever you're ready."

"I'll leave you, then." Alicia blew a kiss as she backed away. "Prayers and best wishes, my friend."

Julia closed the door behind her, then turned to Maddie with an encouraging smile. "Ready for your veil?"

She studied her reflection in the mirror. "I think I'm going to skip it after all. Witt and I have no secrets between us, and he's already seen me at my best and worst."

"I am so happy for you." Julia tucked a stray lock into the pearl-studded butterfly clip holding Maddie's curls in place.

Hearing the crack in her friend's voice, Maddie turned and drew her into a hug. "I pray every day that you'll be this happy again, too."

"Stop!" Julia eased away and flicked a finger beneath each eyelid. "This is *your* day. It's time to go out there and marry your sweetheart."

Nervously stroking Ranger, Witt peered down the hallway. Would his bride ever make an appearance?

Maybe she'd gotten cold feet. Maybe she'd changed her mind. Maybe—

Julia peeked around the corner with a nod and a thumbs-up, and the harpist made a smooth segue into "Be Thou My Vision," the hymn they'd chosen for the processional.

With a hand on Witt's shoulder, Carl, his best man, guided him into position in front of Pastor Peters. "Take a breath. It's gonna be fine."

Once he glimpsed Maddie, dazzlingly beautiful in her white gown, everything *was* fine. Better than fine. Perfect in every way.

From that moment on, everything became a blur, until…

"Ladies and gentlemen," the pastor announced amid applause, laughter and a happy bark from Ranger, "I present Mr. and Mrs. Angus Nathaniel Wittenbauer."

Taken aback at the use of his full name, he looked at Maddie askance. "I thought we'd agreed—"

"I know," she whispered close to his ear, "but it's my name, too, now, and I'm proud of it. Proud of *you*."

After a flurry of best wishes and congratulations, the guests who weren't staying for dinner said their goodbyes. Maddie donned an apron—she'd refused to change out of her gorgeous wedding gown—and with Julia's help served dinner. Witt felt it a special honor to stand at the head of the table and carve the roast.

Later, he insisted on taking over kitchen cleanup. With his tux coat off and shirtsleeves rolled up, he filled the sink.

Trent came up beside him. "Let me help, Dad."

"Thanks, son." Having his kids with him made this day even more meaningful. He'd worried it might be awkward including Linda and Ed, but instead, their supportive presence brought closure for the past…and affirmation for this new beginning. He'd already enjoyed a few opportunities to reconnect with Trent and Emily and looked forward to many more—and for Maddie to get to know them better, too.

God bless her for never giving up. Oh, how he loved that woman!

Sniffling, he swiped his sleeve across his eyes.

"Dad? Hey, it's okay." Trent handed him a towel. "Go be with your bride. I'll get Kurt to help me finish in here."

He found her deep in conversation with Linda and Emily. They were smiling and laughing—a good sign—but when they looked his way and immediately went silent, he could only wonder what they'd been saying about him.

"Hi, honey." Eyes sparkling, Maddie took his hand. "Is everything all right?"

"I just missed you, is all." He lowered his voice. "Can we get out of here for a few minutes?"

"Of course."

In the mudroom, he helped her into her puffy down jacket, then slipped on his own while she traded her wedding shoes for fleece-lined boots. With Ranger following close behind, they stepped out beneath a slightly overcast sky, snow flurries floating on the northerly February breeze. Witt wrapped his bride beneath his arm, and they strolled across the yard.

It seemed natural to find themselves at the kennel. Holding the door for Maddie, Witt beamed at her. "This is where my life truly began."

She caressed his cheek. "No, my darling, because if not for everything that had gone before, we'd never have met. We are who we are because of all our yesterdays."

He pondered that for a moment and knew she was right. "Then it's a good thing we worship a merciful God who specializes in redeeming the past."

"So, how about we get started on our amazing future?" She seized his lapels and drew him forward.

They kissed, and might never have come up for air if a certain dog hadn't set every canine in the building to barking. Witt couldn't be sure if the dogs were celebrating with them or just wanted supper. Both, he decided, because this was his family, and just like those precious pups, he'd found his forever home.

* * * * *

Dear Reader,

As a life-long dog lover, I enjoy so much including special canines in my stories. Steadfast and quick to forgive, dogs are perhaps the truest earthly examples of God's unconditional love. They also model how we as God's children can trust in His benevolent mercy and rely on Him for every need.

Even when we think our faith is strong, as Witt did, we may have blind spots, areas of our lives we haven't fully turned over to the Lord. Those are where we encounter the lessons God most needs to teach us. For Witt, it was embracing his worth as a forgiven child of God. For Maddie, it was learning to trust again and open her heart to love. I imagine the Lord using Ranger, Joey and the other Eventide canines to help their human companions along their journey of growth.

I hope you enjoyed this visit to fictional Elk Valley, Montana. I love hearing from my readers, so please contact me through my website, www.MyraJohnson. com, where you can also subscribe to my e-newsletter.

With prayers and gratitude,
Myra

COMING NEXT MONTH FROM
Love Inspired

PINECRAFT REFUGE
Pinecraft Seasons • by Lenora Worth

Grieving widower Tanner Dawson has no intentions of ever marrying again, but when he meets Eva Miller sparks fly. Giving her a job at his store is the last thing he wants, but he needs the help. As they get closer, can he keep his secrets to protect his daughter?

THE SECRET AMISH ADMIRER
by Virginia Wise

Shy Eliza Zook has secretly been in love with popular Gabriel King since they were children, but he has never noticed her. When a farm injury forces Gabriel to work alongside her in an Amish gift shop, will it be her chance to finally win him over?

REUNITED BY THE BABY
Sunset Ridge • by Brenda Minton

After finding a baby abandoned in the back of his truck, Matthew Rivers enlists the help of RN Parker Smythe, the woman whose love he once rejected. When their feelings start to blossom, could it lead them on a path to something more?

HER ALASKAN RETURN
Serenity Peak • by Belle Calhoune

Back in her hometown in Alaska, single and pregnant Autumn Hines comes face-to-face with first love Judah Campbell when her truck breaks down. Still reeling from tragedy, the widowed fisherman finds hope when he reconnects with Autumn. But can their relationship withstand the secret she's been keeping?

A HOME FOR THE TWINS
by Danielle Thorne

The struggling Azalea Inn is the perfect spot for chef Lindsey Judd to raise her twin boys. But things get complicated when lawyer Donovan Ainsworth comes to stay. Love is the last thing either of them want, but two little matchmakers might feel differently...

HIS TEMPORARY FAMILY
by Julie Brookman

Firefighter Sam Tiernan's life gets turned upside down when a car accident leaves his baby nieces in his care. When his matchmaking grandmother ropes next-door neighbor Fiona Shay into helping him, it might be the push they both need to open their hearts to something more...

LOOK FOR THESE AND OTHER LOVE INSPIRED BOOKS WHEREVER BOOKS ARE SOLD, INCLUDING MOST BOOKSTORES, SUPERMARKETS, DISCOUNT STORES AND DRUGSTORES.

LICNM0223

Get 4 FREE REWARDS!

We'll send you 2 FREE Books plus <u>plus</u> 2 FREE Mystery Gifts.

FREE Value Over **$20**

Both the **Love Inspired**® and **Love Inspired**® **Suspense** series feature compelling novels filled with inspirational romance, faith, forgiveness and hope.

YES! Please send me 2 FREE novels from the Love Inspired or Love Inspired Suspense series and my 2 FREE gifts (gifts are worth about $10 retail). After receiving them, if I don't wish to receive any more books, I can return the shipping statement marked "cancel." If I don't cancel, I will receive 6 brand-new Love Inspired Larger-Print books or Love Inspired Suspense Larger-Print books every month and be billed just $6.49 each in the U.S. or $6.74 each in Canada. That is a savings of at least 16% off the cover price. It's quite a bargain! Shipping and handling is just 50¢ per book in the U.S. and $1.25 per book in Canada.* I understand that accepting the 2 free books and gifts places me under no obligation to buy anything. I can always return a shipment and cancel at any time by calling the number below. The free books and gifts are mine to keep no matter what I decide.

Choose one: ☐ **Love Inspired**
Larger-Print
(122/322 IDN GRHK)

☐ **Love Inspired Suspense**
Larger-Print
(107/307 IDN GRHK)

Name (please print)

Address   Apt. #

City   State/Province   Zip/Postal Code

Email: Please check this box ☐ if you would like to receive newsletters and promotional emails from Harlequin Enterprises ULC and its affiliates. You can unsubscribe anytime.

Mail to the **Harlequin Reader Service:**
IN U.S.A.: P.O. Box 1341, Buffalo, NY 14240-8531
IN CANADA: P.O. Box 603, Fort Erie, Ontario L2A 5X3

Want to try 2 free books from another series! Call 1-800-873-8635 or visit www.ReaderService.com.

HARLEQUIN
PLUS

Try the best multimedia subscription service for romance readers like you!

Read, Watch and Play.

Experience the easiest way to get the romance content you crave.

Start your **FREE TRIAL** at
<u>www.harlequinplus.com/freetrial</u>.